Larry   Peachpie

The
STAY-AWAKE MEN
& Other Unstable Entities
Matthew M. Bartlett

Copyright © 2016 Matthew M. Bartlett

All rights reserved.

ISBN: 1720393648

ISBN-13: 9781720393641

This book is dedicated to Steven W. Kendrick.
I wish he could have been here for this.

C O N T E N T S

BARTLETT AND YOU:
AN UNSAFETY GUIDE

By Scott Nicolay

Y ou may already know what I am going to say here, or at least you may think you do: *Matthew Bartlett is one of those authors whose emergence redefines the genre.* Barker, Ligotti, Barron, Llewellyn... Bartlett. And there I said it. Not that it will come as any surprise to you if you have read *Gateways to Abomination* and/or *Creeping Waves*...his importance is really a given at this point.

That's really only a starting point though, isn't it? It may well be the reason why you are here in the first place. You may have heard the rumors. You may think you know it already. You may even think you know what you are in for with this latest collection of his work.

But things are never what they seem chez Bartlett, are they? If you have played previously in his twisted playground (a setting he actually used in one of the most memorable stories from *Gateways*) you might anticipate a progression from creepy to disturbing to holy-shit-what-the-fuck, followed by a long hot shower and gargling with salt water to get the taste of pus and leeches out of your mouth (it won't work, trust me). Critic s.j. bagley has described this payload delivery system of The Weird and its lingering effects as *unsettlement*...a deceptively understated term, especially in Bartlett's case. He works like a decrepit Charon ferrying readers from the shores of the self to the *unself*, boatloads at a time, and for mere pennies. Each of his stories is a kind of haunted house that shunts you through multiple unexpected turns and shocks, rapidly deranging your narrative expectations until...it doesn't really matter because the you who entered is no longer the reader who emerges.

Just so does my friend Matthew defy expectations afresh with each new tale. The reader cannot possibly know what you did going in because you never came out. Not that such knowledge would be much help anyway. Bartlett's narratives follow no formula, not even their own. Every story is a unique labyrinth with its own rules, or rather, his labyrinth has no rules. Its corridors and catacombs are constantly shifting, ceaselessly changing, always Bartlett, never the same. There are many points of entry. No way out.

Here the reader, searching for some fixed reference, a place to attach one end of a long skein of colored yarn, may proclaim triumphantly: "But Bartlett's stories all *do* have a common thread: WXXT, the sinister and mysterious radio station operated by an ancient and even more mysterious witch cult in Leeds, Massachusetts!"

So the reader may think...but that reader is neither you nor me. And the reader who is fortunate enough to have acquired a copy of this small volume is about to discover that our protean author has, like the slime mold, shifted into a new form and slithered on to new ground during the dark intervals of our eye blinks. You can't step into the same Bartlett twice.

Oh, he is not without form, but no one has seen his true form. Though not all Weird writers are evolving, Bartlett, like rust, plasmodia, or The Weird itself, never rests. A certain type of reader might attempt to create a visual representation of the current amorphous state of The Weird, assigning a set of variable characteristics to each author and mapping our work along multiple axes in three or more dimensions. Such a display would likely reveal an overlapping array of lumpy blobs, many clustered closely together in unwholesome familiarity, others positioned at some greater remove from the crowd. Bartlettia would be one of the latter.

A similar approach to each individual author's corpus might produce similar results, showing nuclear cores surrounded by more elastic pseudopodia extending in new directions. Variation within many populations would inevitably stand revealed as greater than that between the populations themselves. And within that dark star map, a graphic representation of the seven tale subset that comprises *The Stay-Awake Men and Other Stories* would indeed portray a single cluster and that cluster would still lie within the overall Bartlettosphere. These tale all give me that Bartlett Fink Feeling, true--but they belong to a new and distinct extrusion of that system. Of course it is no secret that Bartlett is going places. He always has been. Just not the places the reader expects.

So it is with *The Stay-Awake Men and Other Stories* (six other stories, to be exact): WXXT remains silent here. Leeds receives mention more than once--as does its major employer, Annelid Industries International--but though these are all distinctly Bartlett stories, none of them are "Leeds stories." The titular tale is actually set at a radio station--but not WXXT. The *différance* is quite delicious, really. Amidst the familiar flavors in this batch of stew are tantalizing hints of Barker, Ligotti, Aickman, Samuels, and Klein, stronger than they have been before, but not strong enough to do more than add spice to the stock of an author who himself seems to grow in power with every paragraph. "Spettrini" (which previously appeared as a limited edition chapbook from Dunhams Manor Press) in particular invoked not only "The Glamour," a long-standing personal favorite among Ligotti's tales, but also Barker's *Imajica*. Perhaps that was just me, but there is no way for me to tell now.

The Stay-Awake Men shows Bartlett not simply shifting his territory, but broadening it overall, becoming a little more literary perhaps, maybe a bit more strange or uncanny, as some prefer to style it in the Other England, the "Old" one. Part of that must come from the extent that the author has distopiated these tales, distancing them from one of the most distinctive locales in contemporary fiction. While the reader was distracted, Bartlett expanded, growing not only greater, but nearer. As his tales become less *local*, they become more *universal*. Was there a vacant house down the street from you? It may have a new occupant. Don't worry if you can't visit: it may come to you.

Oh look, here in your hands: it has already arrived. Oh well, time for me to leave. It was nice knowing you.

Bartlett's house has many doors. Many gateways in. No way out. Don't worry though. I think you will like it there.

CARNOMANCER, OR THE MEAT MANAGER'S PREROGATIVE

LaFogg stared down through the two-way mirror at the new ginger-haired cashier as she bent to retrieve a coupon that had fallen from the dispenser. She was far too young for him to be ogling, he thought, but damned if she didn't strongly resemble a younger iteration of KaraLee, his former wife, down to the spray of freckles across the back of her slender neck. She was going to grow up tall, he thought. Rangy. *Leggy*.

He was on the ugly side of his fifties, a mere half-inch taller than very short, with a protruding belly and a bald spot that stayed resolutely pink no matter the season: not exactly the kind of man the cashier would ever look at with anything other than indifference or even, he allowed, mild disgust. A noise escaped his mouth as she bent further and he saw the eye-shaped patch of pale skin between her store-issued yellow polo and her black leggings.

One of the customers in her line, a stooped, elderly man in a flat cap and windbreaker, looked up toward the offices and LaFogg reflexively took a step back. He knew no one could see through the glass, but the old creep appeared to be looking right at him. He sat back down at his desk, opened up the quarterly sales report, and pretended to stare at it. The speaker above his desk squelched, and an electronic code sounded: three blips in rapid succession, a pause, and a fourth. A disruption on the floor. He grabbed the armrests of his chair and hoisted himself up, padded down the stairs as the voice of Grant, the assistant manager, came over the loudspeaker, *An associate to Department 9 for customer assistance please. Department 9. Customer assistance.*

Department 9 was Meats, located at the back of the store, opposite the registers. LaFogg walked briskly down the cereal aisle, occasionally breaking into a shambling, arrhythmic travesty of a jog. The bottom of his yellow shirt came untucked, flapping like a flag. An angled shopping cart blocked his way, helmed by a short Spanish lady intently comparing the Cap'n Crunch ingredients with those of Admiral Crispy, the market's version. LaFogg sucked in his gut, squeezed by. A crowd had begun to form at the end of the aisle. He pushed through them, and then stopped short.

Crouched in the meat case that stretched between the deli and the dairy case was a baldheaded man. He looked to be in his forties, was barefoot, built like a professional wrestler, clad in checkered pants and a white apron stained pink with ghosts of bloodstains. His had monstrous arms carpeted with thick, wiry hair. LaFogg noticed a price sticker pinched into the man's prodigious black mustache. With both hands he was lustily prying the cellophane from a huge hunk of bottom-round roast. Scattered across the tan and white tiled floor were torn shards of Styrofoam, sheets of pink-stained padding, and bunched remnants of cellophane, bubbled pink with blood. They looked to LaFogg like the sloughed-off skins of snakes. Among them sat the man's shoes, placed evenly side by side, one black sock neatly folded in each.

LaFogg fumbled through a mental catalog of things to say, but came up empty. His mouth opened and closed. He held out his arms, and realized he hadn't planned anything in particular for them to do. He let them fall back to his side and settled for arranging his face into an affronted expression. Two policemen pushed past him.

"Sir," shouted the taller of the two. "Climb down out of there and get down on the floor."

The man grinned at them, revealing bright white, gleaming teeth, as though from a toothpaste commercial. His mustache, by contrast, was so black it appeared to have been dyed. "It's in here somewhere," he said. "It has to be in here somewhere." With that, he turned his attention back to the roast. He began tearing it open with his hands, digging in his nails, pulling it apart. The policemen descended upon him, hooked their arms through his, and hauled him up out of the case. The roast fell to the floor with a moist thump. One cop forced the man to the ground and wrenched his arms behind his back. The other knelt on his legs and cuffed him. The man cried out, a howl of frustrated rage, and thrust out a hand toward the roast, muscles straining, perfect teeth clenched. Then he looked at LaFogg. And smiled.

Rekka, one of the deli men, blonde-haired, squinty eyed and slouchy, came over and stood at LaFogg's side. Rekka surveyed the scene, looking from where the policemen were hoisting the man up to his feet, past the pink and red wreckage in the meat case, down to the tattered cellophane on the floor, then back, over the faces of the gathered crowd. He was grinning avidly. "Who *is* that?" LaFogg said.

"That," Rekka said, "is Foxcroft. He is the Meat Manager." He laughed. "*Was* the Meat Manager."

"*I've* never seen him here," LaFogg said.

"He's been here, like, forever," said Rekka.

It was mid-December. The first snow of the season had fallen the week before, and three consecutive 40-degree days melted most of it away. All that remained was brown-topped hillocks of pebble-pimpled snow gathered at the curbs like trash. The landscape was a hundred muddy shades of brown, fallen leaves, denuded trees, dirt-dusted blacktop, brown-bricked houses squatting like frogs in a polluted pond, all of it domed by a cadaver-grey sky. LaFogg piloted his Caprice through the maze of parking lots and dumpsters and boulder-strewn landscaping, then onto Haines Boulevard, a long, ruler-straight street of three-story apartment houses where dead trees moped along the curb and intermittent fences of varying poor quality bracketed front yards overgrown or barren. LaFogg could tell which was his by the tree in front, the one doubled over as though in unbearable pain.

LaFogg's eave-angled bedroom was lit blue by the moonlight outside: his small bed, its sheets twisted, the nightstand beside it, the dresser at its foot crowned by a dusty-screened 14-inch television. It was 7 p.m., early, and he wasn't due back at the market until 11 the next day. Nevertheless, he undressed to his V-neck and his Fruit of the Looms, untied the knot of covers, and reclined on the bed, back to the wall. He groped for the remote and found it under the arch of his knee.

He started flipping rapidly through the channels—*how do you even register what you're seeing?* KaraLee used to ask—when somewhere in there a flash of female flesh caught his eye. He flipped back through the channels until he found it: a shapely brunette with white angelic wings, standing before a red chaise lounge, black curtains undulating in slow-motion behind her. She wore a sheer white negligee, short, hemmed with lace. The broad sweep of the wings spreading behind her, framing her figure, set LaFogg's imagination into motion: how the contours of her body would feel against his back as they soared over the city, her talons gripping his undershirt. She ran her hand along the curve of her hip, then down the length of her leg, crouching slightly, staring at the camera. Her lips were red, full, wet. A toll-free number appeared at the bottom of the screen. *Call me*, the woman said. *I'm waiting. I'm so lonely here. Everyone has gone. It is gone. Do you have it? It has to be in here somewhere.*

She turned and strode over to the chaise lounge, knelt on it, and began clawing at its seam, her rump up in the air, a high-heeled shoe dangling from her foot. That foot was filthy: there was mud smeared across her heel and caked between her toes like plaque. The sounds of the tearing, of rending, were terribly loud. He thumbed the volume down a few notches. The camera swam in and out of focus, and he saw that the chaise lounge was composed of large chunks of raw meat, veined and lined with white, glistening fat. The woman, possessed of a brutish strength, was splitting connective tissue, shredding the meat to bloody strips. The screen blurred to pixels, and came back into focus to reveal the woman's appleskin-red lips spanning the little Sony. LaFogg could see the pores, the pink, stratified skin, the fine hairs of her face above the cupid's bow. *Call me*, she whispered. *Call me now.*

The phone number seemed to ripple as the curtains continued to flutter in the background. LaFogg's eyelids twitched, he let out a honk of a snore, and then he was in the room with the chaise lounge. The woman was gone. The curtains, still fluttering, parted to reveal the door that led to the butcher shop in the market. From somewhere beyond came a buzzing, as of insects in a state of agitation. LaFogg pushed his way through, felt his way through the familiar darkened corridor, lined with pallets. Ahead he saw a light rendered funereally grey by opaque plastic flaps. He divided them with his hands and pushed his way through into the workroom, held up his hand against the now harsh light.

The walls were white, dimpled in a cinquefoil pattern, damp from a new washing. Fatigue mats lined the floors in front of the work surfaces. At the far end of the room in a white smock and apron stood Foxcroft, his features obscured by a cap and a surgical mask. He was running a whirring blade down a column of grey meat, sheets of it falling at his feet. He turned, pulled down his mask, and silenced the electric knife. *It has to be in here somewhere*, he said, and his voice echoed around the room, each iteration slower and deeper than the last, until it was just a sepulchral drone. He turned and walked through a doorway to his right. LaFogg followed. In the next room, hanging from a metal rack by a hook through her feet, was the woman from the sex line commercial. She was flayed to the muscle, her skin piled off to the side like discarded clothing. Her wings hung dampened, limp, and stained red. The last of her blood was dripping from her body into an overflowing metal tray. Blood pooled in the center of the room, slowly spiraling down into a floor-spanning line of feather-clogged drains. Foxcroft drew from his smock a large chef's knife and began hacking at the base of one of the wings. *It has to be in here somewhere*, he screamed, as blood sprayed in powerful, pulsing jets.

LaFogg awoke, kicked the covers away from him. The room was awash in light from the snowy television screen. He heard voices in the white noise, whispering to him. *Go to the window*, they said. *Look and see. Look and see.* He went to the window, put his hands on the cold glass, and looked out into the night. On the curb across the road was a man, tall, with a substantial belly like an overfilled pastry, his long overcoat unable to fully suppress its girth. He had a prodigious brown beard that the wind tossed about like a tree of dead leaves. Fists at his hips, he appeared to be striking a heroic pose, like a Viking at the helm of some great ship. As LaFogg watched, the man began to dance. It was a mournful dance, slow and deliberate, with no discernible pattern. To the sibilant music of the night he swayed, reached up his hands, shimmied, ducked, and twirled. His grace belied his heft. He was positioned between two yellow circles of streetlights. His features were hidden in shadows. No cars passed. The man danced and danced. LaFogg felt a hollow and howling feeling of tremendous loss surge up from the pit of his gut and climb the length of his spine. He yanked down the ragged, browned shade and returned to bed.

He fell instantly to sleep.

⸻

Three weeks later LaFogg sat in the break room, sliding the tines of his fork around the edges of a black plastic tray, prying up browned remnants of a Stouffer's Macaroni & Cheese. The holidays were over and the workload had eased. Most of the staff had bounced back, gossiping with perverse enthusiasm, complaining about customers, smoking outside in chattering clusters, but he seemed to be stuck in a spiral of exhaustion, a despair whose source was a mystery to him. If someone came into the office where he was, he jumped as though a gunshot had gone off. When he woke in the mornings, he wished nothing more than to be unconscious again. He scraped off some burnt brown cheese and pushed it between his back teeth. The door behind him opened and Rekka came around and dropped into a chair across from him as though having fallen from a great height. "So!" he said. "Remember Foxcroft?"

"The Meat Manager," LaFogg said. "I haven't seen anything in the paper about it."

"Check this out," said Rekka, and he reached into his jacket pocket and pulled out a folded flyer.

At the top of the white sheet was a photocopied image of a Polaroid of Foxcroft, massive, muscled arms folded over his chest, staring into the camera with a malevolent intensity. The copy was dark, so most of his features were obscured in black ink, but the flyaway brows and the mustache were evident, as was the gleam of his bald pate. Below the picture was the following:

FOXCROFT
I was born with a great gift, and have honed it with intensive study in the OCCULT SCIENCES of CARNOMANCY and BIBLIOMANCY

Love, Work, Luck, Family, Business
Legal Matters
I will read and interpret your OMENS!
The most effective JADOO!
AVENGE a loved one! AVENGE yourself!
I am your PORTAL! SEE THE RED WORLD
BEHIND OURS!

LaFogg looked at the shadowy figure on the flyer. "Can I have this?" he said.

"There's one on your car," Rekka said. "There's one on every car in the lot."

⸺

That night after his shift LaFogg drove to Foxcroft's shop. He had no idea what he might do when he got there. Maybe just take a look inside. Maybe get a cheap reading done, to satisfy his curiosity. The building was one that he recognized as having recently housed a Verizon Wireless outlet. It was a wide set A-frame house with an open porch fronted by four steel columns. The word PSYCHIC in massive red spot-lit letters spanned the second floor facade, the first C nearly enclosing a porthole emanating ivory light. The two ground floor windows bore neon representations of yellow eyes on a purple crescent moon, of a green head split in two with an orange cow skull visible in the fissure, of a red hand with the middle and forefinger raised. Behind the windows, the spotless louvered blinds lay slightly open, angled upward.

He opened the outside door and entered a small anteroom. To his left sat a white wicker couch with flowered cushions, a glass-topped coffee table, also of white wicker, with a vase of flowers. Ahead stood a solid white door with a peephole, adjacent to that, a doorbell, which LaFogg rang. Somewhere within, chimes sounded.

The door opened a crack, a female eye appeared, the lid red-lashed and freckled. As she pulled open the door,

LaFogg recognized her as the redheaded cashier. The room behind her was larger than it had seemed possible from the outside. There were racks of candles, many melted down, only a few lit. The shop reeked of dueling incense aromas with an undercurrent of smoked meat. On another set of shelves sat a variety of disparaged stone Buddhas in aspects of derangement and disfigurement and horror. Some were small as mice; the largest was the size of a fat housecat. To a piece the carving was precisely and exquisitely detailed. Some of the figures had torn earlobes eroding at the edges. The robes of a few were littered with scattered teeth under an anguished gummy grimace. In one or two, that grimace bore a violently truncated tongue. Some had split skulls from whose ragged gashes sprung bubbles and some unknown manner of sprouts. One large red figure's chubby cheeks were torn like paper, revealing striated muscle beneath. Stuck in its forehead was a cluster of porcupine quills; its eyes, somewhat crossed, looked upward in abjection.

To the right of the display from a thick rope depended clusters of sausages, like the many-fingered fists of some unknown species of giant. Settled into their gray skins like a profusion of warts were a variety of stones and crystals: chalcopyrite, speckled with the colors of autumn; ocean-hued lapis; purple ametrine; rutilated quartz that looked like fine hairs caught in a congealed bubble. A standing fan, its blades grey with dust, pointed at them, causing them to undulate slightly, the stones clicking together in tinny percussion.

Mounted on the wall in the far corner was a grotesque cow's head, untouched by even the rudest taxidermy. Its eyes, red and rheumy, bulged from their sockets, its mouth hung open, crowded with a swelled and split tongue that pushed up against its teeth, and LaFogg could see the bullet hole that had ended its life, ringed with singed fur. Maggots squirmed in its flared nostrils while flies buzzed about it. He felt something plummet in his stomach.

"I… I should go," he said. The girl smiled, shook her

head, and reached for his hand to grasp it. He took her hand into his instead. He hadn't intended to do so. She frowned, but did not pull away. Her hand was small and cold, and he held it lightly, between his fingers and thumb, as one might hold a baby bird rescued from a snow drift. She led him to a corner of the room sectioned off by diaphanous white curtains. She pulled aside a section of fabric and hooked it to the wall, and he entered to see two folding chairs facing each other, between them a white cloth-covered table bearing a covered platter. On the back of the nearest chair was a scribble of marker indicating that it was from the nondenominational church a block south, the one KaraLee used to attend against LaFogg's wishes. The cashier motioned her hand at the chair, and he sat.

"He will be along in a matter of moments," she said in a soft, shy voice, and LaFogg felt a jolt of fear touch his spine like the cold point of a knife.

She was gone. He shivered in the frigid cold of the room. He put his hands on the edges of the chair to lift himself, to leave, when Foxcroft ducked in and swiftly sat. He was wearing all black, some kind of linen robe that looked almost like a Karate outfit. LaFogg wondered that the chair could hold him. "I know you," said Foxcroft.

Though it wasn't a question, LaFogg felt pressed to answer. "I'm the front-end manager at Foster's."

"Of course," Foxcroft said, not sounding at all surprised. "Oh, Mister La*Fogg*. Such insights await you." His voice was unaccented, thin, as though emitting from the cheap speaker of a transistor radio. "You've always been so close to the other side. Have you felt it?"

LaFogg had not, but he thought it would be rude to say so. "I have," he said.

"No, no, you haven't." Foxcroft said, smiling. He was missing two teeth. "But that doesn't mean a thing. You have walked so close to the rift. If you couldn't smell it, it could you. Something is missing for you, yes?"

LaFogg thought of KaraLee. What had become of her?

He had blocked out his memory of her for so long. Had she left him? Or was it he who had left? He pictured her face distorted by tears, her voice pleading for him to stop, just stop, please stop. He opened his mouth and what came out was, "The girl who opened the door for me, who brought me in…"

Foxcroft pushed his lips back from his teeth. "Nobody brought you in," he said. "You rang the bell, and I buzzed you in."

"Was it KaraLee?"

"It was no one, Mister LaFogg. No one at all."

He reached out and lifted the cover from the platter, his eyes fixed on LaFogg's eyes. Underneath sat an oblong chunk of meat. "Put your hands on this."

LaFogg put his hands on either side of the meat. Foxcroft rested his massive hands over his. They were cold as snow. *What is it*, whispered Foxcroft. *What is hiding under the stairs inside your head?* He began to chant, to sing, in some unknown language. LaFogg clutched the meat in his hands. Images fluttered around him like butterflies: holding KaraLee's long red hair under his nose like a mustache…a snowdrift, pink with blood…winged cashiers, their heads bent in prayer under lit, numbered halos…severed hands on Styrofoam platters, trapped under taut blankets of cellophane, trying to dig their way out.

Oh, we are in the thick of it now, in the marrow, in the throes, Foxcroft said. The red neon from outside shone on his head, giving it the appearance of a gaudy bulb. *We are truly in the head of the long bone.* He grabbed the chunk of meat from between LaFogg's hands and hurled it at the wall, then grabbed LaFogg by the shoulders of his shirt, lifted him and spun him around.

The wall was all meat, red, bifurcated vertically with a labial line of white deckle.

GO, Foxcroft demanded, and LaFogg went to the wall and put his hands to it.

It felt cool to the touch, just slightly damp. He dug his

fingernails into the deckle, pushing the meat to either side, tearing at the cartilage, forcing it open. It was cold under his nails. His muscles ached with the strain. He bowed his head and used it to push further through the meat, while his hands pushed to widen the gap and his right foot stomped downward. He pushed himself in all the way. The wall closed behind him and he was enwombed, the red and pink and white pushing in at him from all sides. The smell of raw meat, of blood, was bright and blue in his nostrils. He continued to push, tearing, the meat yielding, the spongy sinew splitting, he pushed and he pushed and tore with his hands and his head and his knees.

And then he was out.

The room was a mirror image of the one he'd left, but the floor and all of the walls were red, marbled with bright white sinew. The curtains were silverskin, the bone dome on the skeletal table resting on a platter of paillard. Behind the bone chair stood Foxcroft—or, rather, Foxcroft's skeleton. Swirling in complex orbits around it were intestines like a writhing nest of snakes, a pulsating liver, clouds of fat, his brain circuiting his bare skull on a stiff lasso of spinal column. LaFogg lifted the dome off of the platter to find Foxcroft's face, folded like a washcloth, an eyeless lid gaping at the top. Next to it was a length of tongue, tied in a knot at its root.

Go home, said Foxcroft.

Home, thought LaFogg. What was *home* on this side of the wall? Would KaraLee be there? Or the angel from the television, wings unfolding wetly, tearing away from the body like fat pulled from flesh, fanning out behind her in preparation for flight?

LaFogg opened the door, walked through the red anteroom, and stepped out into the world. Above was a ceiling of strips of white fat split by yellow ribbons of backstrap, beyond which lay degraded sky bloomed cherry, interrupted by distorted half-moons of connective tissue. Ahead, cars like butterflied cutlets rumbled on purple tournedos, navigating the red roads, bouncing through tissue-ringed abscesses. Above swooped squalls of ganglia, lighting here and there, browning the surface of whatever they touched. LaFogg walked past buildings that were sawed and squared roasts, under bridges of bone from which depended rags of torn muscle. To his left seethed the river, all roiling pink exudate. Numerous times he slid as though on ice. Before long he attained Haines Street, its houses stacked like brochettes with windows of glistening marrow. His own building, fronted by a doubled-over cluster of intestines, was tinged here and there with blue-green iridescence where in the other world there had been a tangle of vines.

He squirmed up the slippery stairs, pulling himself forward by his nails. His apartment was brightly lit, crowded with skeletons pouring cocktails into their jaws and down their ribs like grim fountains, ice cubes tumbling like boulders down the staircases of ivory bone. The cadavers cackled and gibbered as they navigated the floor of piled wings, feathers withered and black with blood. The woman from the sex line commercial lay face-down on the futon, the feathers gone from her wings, all that remained of them jointed black tines like the skeleton of an umbrella. He turned, and there was KaraLee, shredded and shorn and dead, one of her gnarled hands resting maternally on the rotting shoulder of the ginger-haired cashier, the other on the rotting shoulder of Rekka. The three grinned at him brainlessly. Their skin was sloughing off of their bodies, puddling damply around them like discarded grey skirts. A terrible sound filled the room, a cacophony of buzzing insects, whirring blades, white nose. Foxcroft emerged from the crowd, his jaw hanging to his collarbone, his organs constellating about him, the electric knife vibrating in his huge hands. He ran it down LaFogg's body, and again, and again. He decorated the room.

Outside, in the street, under the night sky, the bearded man danced and danced.

Monica, the ginger-haired cashier, sat in the break room playing Words With Friends on her phone. Stan, the deli guy, pushed the door open and slouched into the room.

"Did you hear about the front-end manager? LaFogg?"

Monica did not look up from her phone. "Crazy," she said. "To do that to someone."

"I know," said Stan. "And she was…"

"Yeah. With twins, too."

"And then to turn himself in, after five years. I mean, like, he'd gotten away with it. Guilt, maybe? They said he was 'insensible.'"

Monica put down her phone. "He always looked at me funny, you know," she said. "Gave me the creeps."

.

SPETTRINI

*K*etter Greyson was an illusionist by trade, schooled and experienced in all of the attendant disciplines and varieties of performance, but if there was a trick to aging elegantly, or at least gracefully, it was one he was unable to master. While the Great Spettrini, his mentor, before disappearing amidst rumors of deviltry and dark doings, had affected a patriarchal, authoritative manner and a pointed Van Dyke beard of solid white, Greyson had grown paunchy and raspy, tentative and hesitant. His hair, which at one time he could sweep up into an imposing pompadour, had grown thin and wispy. His eyebrows, once tools of suggestion and dark insinuation, had become as overgrown and unruly as black thatch on a blighted landscape.

In the waning years of his life, Greyson carried on his person at all times a 19th century Sheffield dagger eight and one half inches long encased in a scabbard of red leather. The handle was said to have been made of bone, specifically from the femur of a 119-year old magician still performing nightly in Prague. On the not infrequent occasions that Greyson performed in an unfamiliar venue or a private home, before entering, it was his custom to leap to the doorjamb, thrust the dagger's blade into it, and lurch back, his hands raised in an aspect of defense and defiance. He would deduct from his fee the cost of the repair. One may find among his papers, housed in the archives of the Leeds

Public Library, a weathered but still legible carbon copy of a contract with the Leeds Academy of Music which says as much. The practice was thought by many to have been an affectation, a peccadillo, or simply a mark of the man's eccentricity. In point of fact, the custom was more significant than that.

Greyson the Great sprawled in the hotel bed face down as if hurled there, and he dreamed. A grey fog hung in the air just above a filthy river lined with sagging trees, as though it were the river's spirit looking down upon its dying body. Old ladies in nightgowns were being swept helplessly along by the flood-swollen waters, and their rescuers, gruff old men in sheriff's uniforms and hats, were pulling them onto the shore by their sagging, veined arms, calling them "goddamned fools." Greyson himself stood on the shoreline in his underwear, crying, not for the women, but from embarrassment at his exposed paleness and flab. The mud covered his feet. He freed the big toe of his right foot, then his left. They popped from the mud. *Plorp. Plorp.* He stirred, awakened, flipped himself onto his back with considerable and vocal effort. The hotel room was unbearably hot. He would have written it off as haunted if not for having been taught that ghosts bring cold, not heat, to their haunts. He exited the bed, feet finding his slippers, and stepped into the hall, with its faded carpet and cracked wallpaper, to catch a cross-breeze, and indeed found one, though it was anemic and smelled vaguely of mold.

Greyson had traveled a long distance to this unfamiliar

village after having been hired by telephone to perform at a child's birthday party. The voice on the other end of the line had been brisk and businesslike. The caller had inquired as to Greyson's fee and promptly offered double. In his younger days, the offer might have set bells of alarm chiming, but gigs had of late been sparse, and he was in arrears on his rent, his housing depending largely on the nearly exhausted generosity of his landlord, who was, thankfully, very much enamored of "artistic types." The party was not scheduled until midnight—late, especially for a child's party, but Greyson was no parent, so what did he know? His children were cooing doves, sniffing rabbits, and young female assistants in leotards, none of whom knew from bedtime.

Driving at dusk on a long rural road that paralleled the interstate, he had first seen the town, through a break in the thick forest, as a garland of twinkling yellow lights. The tree-lined road on which he was driving was devoid of streetlights until it emerged from the woods; after that point the occasional low cottage or trailer hunkered in the vapor glow, and then, after a hairpin turn, he found himself on a silent yellow-lit main strip cramped with businesses and unfamiliar restaurants, all caged and shackled despite the early hour. If not for the occasional hooded figure sitting in a doorway or meandering along a sidewalk, he might have thought he'd wandered into a still picture. There was no recognizable chain store or familiar corporate logo, save the yellow and red Shell sign impaled on a long pole many yards above a shack of a gas station, glowing like a blood-smeared moon.

The hotel was one street over from where the man on the phone had said it would be. The three-story clapboard building leaned like a drunk against a large, gnarled oak; in fact, the ancient tree had pushed itself up through a portion of the third floor balcony and had consumed a length of the railing. The institution was presided over by a skeletal baroness behind bulletproof glass. She was festooned with dusty scarves and a haphazard constellation of costume jewelry. She looked like a diseased Christmas tree. He afforded her neither courtesy nor conversation as he perfunctorily filled in and signed with his curving, ornate G the various forms required of him. She pulled from a hook a diamond shaped bit of plastic with the number 184 scrawled on it in marker; from it depended a small copper-colored key. She pushed it over to him, and only then did she tear away her gaze from the adding machine that squatted in front of her like a flattened frog.

"I want that room ex*act*ly the way you found it when you leave," she said, her voice tattered from years of filterless cigarettes.

Greyson raised an eyebrow. "I assure you I have no plans other than to sleep and to leave," he said.

"I know your kind, and you had best mind your step." She glanced down at his attaché and his wheeled case of tricks. "I wish you'd never come," she said, and she did not sound angry. She sounded sad.

After a period of wandering the maze of hallways, he found himself back at Room 184. The room was equipped with a small television, tethered to the wall with a metallic arm with wires for veins. He turned it on. A blandly handsome television host hopped on one foot onto a gaudy set with a cityscape backdrop. The host acknowledged the cacophonous house band, pumping his arms and using his fingers for six-shooters. The bandleader, an elderly man with cataracts, clothed in a loosely tied blue bathrobe, shot back with one finger, ducking slightly behind his synthesizer keyboard. The host strode forward until his head hit the camera, leaving a sweaty blur on the lens.

He backed up, grinning wildly. "Have you heard this," he asked. "Have you heard this, have you seen this, have you read this in the newspaper; did someone whisper this to you from a darkened doorway, from the hair-clogged shower drain in a condemned motel, from the tiny mouth of an anthill in a parking lot? Did the sultry but affected waitress hand you this on a grease-stained note with your check, did the leering priest mutter this to an indifferent congregation of layabouts, did the wind whisper this through the trees as you drove through the burnt remains of a forest, did a radio host intone this news from an ocean of static..." and on and on in such a manner until Greyson finally switched off the set, despite having had a desire to see the first guest, a movie star who had just lost his wife and baby daughters to the new and rampant strain of influenza.

Bereft of the television, he pulled from his attaché a few of his newly received catalogs. He began to flip through the flimsy pages, considering new illusions to add to his act: the Suit of Snakes, the Crying Dwarf, the Decapitation Hat, the Cabinet of Catastrophe. But he could find no inspiration. He consulted his wristwatch for the time, only to discover that the red second hand and the black minute hand had fallen and were resting in the form of a squashed X at the base of the glass. He could tell by the position of the hour hand that it was just past eleven o'clock. He resolved to dress, get a bite, and arrive in time to set up.

A few moments later Greyson stood before the full-length bathroom mirror, resplendent in glittery blue tuxedo top, orange bow-tie, and black cummerbund topping black pinstriped trousers. His shoes were blacked and shined, his hair glued in black lines against his skull, his brows and widow's peak subtly accented with eyebrow pencil. He warped his face into a demented grin, shot his eyebrows up quickly, one after the other, and then sank them down slowly. His dentures shone blindingly white, eyes tinted a devilish red with contact lenses.

Greyson had become interested in magic not because of having seen a performance nor perused a book, but because of a poster. In a glass display adjacent to the door of the Civic Hall, dramatically lit from below, the illustration depicted a long-limbed Spettrini on a field of purple, a gothic iron fence with intertwined skulls and snakes in the foreground and tilting and split gravestones behind him. He was dressed like a vampire, in a tuxedo with a black and red cape, his fingers bent, frozen in mid-gesticulation, his nails black and long. Between his hands a bat hovered upside down in streams of psychic energy, drawn by the artist as one might sketch a range of hillocks. One thin eyebrow was arched and his hair, black as an oil slick on a moonless night, was combed back and plastered flat to his cranium. His mustache was waxed and stuck out from the sides of his face like pipe cleaners. The very words on the poster seized Greyson's imagination. *Enchantments. Levitation. Necromancy. Resurrection.* Its purpose was to advertise Spettrini's upcoming performance at that very hall, a spectacle which Greyson was not to attend, due to the staunch religious beliefs of his parents, Catholics both, who saw all magic as black, as either a tool of the devil or a series of acts of simple chicanery. Even had Spettrini's show not been concerned primarily with the macabre and the outré, he was more likely to be allowed admittance to an abattoir than to a performance of legerdemain and mentalism and illusion.

They could not prevent him, however, from sending letters to the illusionist, and that he did, letters written and rewritten and fretted over as Greyson attempted to find a tone respectful, admiring, but not too fawning. It was not an easy balance to achieve. But something in the missives must have drawn the man's attention, for he agreed to meet with Greyson, to actually depart his home in the Connecticut town of Orford Parish and travel the considerable distance to Leeds.

Spettrini arranged to meet Greyson at The Tunnel Bar, a tavern housed in what had previously been a passageway to and from a now disused train station. Greyson fretted. He would not be admitted due to his age and youthful appearance, he claimed. Spettrini advised him to clear his head of concerns. They met after school on a Thursday. Spettrini ushered the boy in as though they owned the place, they sat and ordered with no questions asked nor identification demanded, and for two hours Spettrini talked with the boy about illusion, about his career, about his philosophies and his theories. Spettrini agreed to come back one Thursday per month, and for some time he kept his word.

The bar was furnished with quartets of oversized leather chairs situated around small tables of brass and glass. The only light came from sparse track lighting along the low, curved ceiling and the votive candles on the tabletops. It was not a place for the claustrophobic. The bar carried sound in strange and unpredictable ways: one might hear a snippet of conversation from ten tables away as clearly as if it were taking place in the immediate proximity. The two would meet at the farthest table, and Spettrini would proffer old handbills, newspaper clippings, and tales of a life of hotels, raucous audiences, and dalliances with dissolute women who'd haunt the door of his dressing room like wraiths. Greyson would sit rapt, drinking expensive cocktails paid for by his mentor, and dream of such a life for himself, far from classroom desks and droning, chalk-fingered schoolteachers.

After nearly eighteen months of meeting, during which Greyson learned not only many illusions, but the histories and controversies behind them, Spettrini abruptly stopped replying to Greyson's letters. Their last meeting had been exciting, but exceedingly unsettling. The great magician had arrived in a state of distraction, his hair uncombed, the corner of his mouth turned down as if stuck that way. His white shirt was stained brown at the collar, and patches of unshaven stubble darkened his face in no discernible pattern. He muttered, repeated himself, ordered a second drink before having started the first. His breath was unsavory, and the alcohol, consumed in heroic quantities, served only to exacerbate the foul miasma. Finally, he'd leaned forward and grabbed Greyson's shirt collar, squeezing it into his fist. "I've had a breakthrough," he said, and his eyes were bright and manic. "Watch."

He leant back and his eyes rolled to the white. His hands gripped the arms of his chair, veins standing out blue and pulsing. A sound went through the room, like that of a heavy glass plate spinning on a marble surface. A wine glass shattered at a table near the entrance, then another. Greyson looked about him and saw that the glass tops of the tables were spinning, faster, faster, sending the candles careening to the walls. The lights flickered and the bottles and glasses clinked faster and faster and Greyson thought for a mad second that his mentor had summoned a ghost-train that would blast through the wall and roar through the tunnel, crushing and damning to nonexistence the few souls within. In the flickering lights, Greyson had a terrible hallucination: for a moment it seemed as though Spettrini's head sent tendrils of flesh back to the chair. Where the tendrils hit the surface, the leather took on the magician's pallor, splotches of flesh spreading like spilled water, and then hair, white and wild, began sprouting from the flesh of the chair. Spettrini reddened, as did the chair, then, as the spinning tables slowed and the stroboscopic effect faded, so did the hallucination.

As the shaken staff rushed about with dustpans and mops, Spettrini released Greyson from his grip, rose from his seat, spun himself into his overcoat, and fled, with Greyson trailing him. Outside a seething and cold rain was pummeling the streets. It was loud on the awning under which they stood. Spettrini said, not bothering to raise his voice over the cacophony, *There is much to learn, boy. There are places other than here, and limits far beyond what anyone has even considered, nor dreamed of exploring.* And then he was in his black car and gone.

After three letters went unanswered, Greyson, standing on a ledge over a pit of despondency, made the decision to get on with his life, to be resolute, to perfect his illusions, to supplant his previous lessons with the solidity and quiet peacefulness of books. He spent his days in the library, his nights peering at illustrations and reading and rereading the biographies of the greats. His first performances were on coffeehouse stages, and they were received with an indifference that bordered on hostility. He supplemented his biographies and books of tricks with several volumes on the topic of public speaking, folded that learning into his routines, and began, slowly, to perfect an act. Once he had taken the step of moving from his parents' home, he flourished.

His first shows, inspired heavily by Spettrini and by famed illusionist Black Herman, featured jars of elixirs and smoking potions in a looming black cabinet set in a landscape of tilting headstones and folded-hand stone angels. Selected audience members would be administered one or another of the "medicines" by a lithe assistant in a black leotard, and after some vamping on Greyson's part, would crumple to the stage as though dead. The doctor of the house, played with a dour seriousness by his older cousin Ernest, would pronounce the poor soul right there on the stage, to the horror of his family members or friends in the audience. The body would be placed into a black casket on the stage, and the audience encouraged to chant a string of nonsense words invented by Ketter as the lights dimmed and shadows flitted in the rafters. The cadaver would then float up through the lid of the coffin and hover above it, spinning slowly, ethereal and ghostlike. Ketter would clap his hands, the house lights would blaze, blinding the audience, and when they dimmed and the crowd's sight returned and the red and blue floating orbs faded from their views, the audience member would be standing behind the coffin, dazed. Two assistants would gingerly help the man back to his seat. Word got around.

A letter arrived at the Greyson household one day several years after Ketter had left. Nicholas Greyson looked at the return address in Connecticut, scowled at the ostentatious handwriting, and tore in two the envelope and the letter within. He deposited it in the trash with the eggshells and the chicken bones and the dust and he never spoke of it to his wife or his son.

Greyson donned his overcoat to shield the street people from his splendor. He swept up his wheeled case, extended the handle, and exited the hotel in search of sustenance. The main street, as before, was shuttered. He passed junk shops, check-cashing establishments, a Gentleman's Club called the Gilded Cardinal. The case bounced in his wake, wheels rumbling on the sidewalks like an extravagant drum roll. He passed a restaurant with white tablecloths, elaborate frescoes of teeming Roman squares, chairs upended on the tables, their limbs raised in the air as though vying to answer a question posed by a hat-stand behind a marble podium. Somewhere in the distance some poor soul launched into a terrible coughing jag punctuated with howling inhalations.

Soon he was beyond the commercial section, among bungalows and one-story clapboard houses, all flickering with the bluish light of televisions, otherwise apparently unlit. Intermittent streetlights provided weak pools of sepia. The bulbs, grouped in fours, were caked in thick dust. At least one of every four had burned out. Bugs swarmed in clouds around them, and from one depended a long web, at the end of which spun a large, dead, dried spider, its legs all touching at their ends, as in a grim ballet. He passed a neglected garden, all tangled vegetation; splintered, split stakes; and sagging string. Somewhere in its dark depths something started and then fled, causing dried and dying leaves to whisper and crunch. As it passed by him, a few stakes toppled, their string pulling down wilted stalks.

Presently he saw a vapor-lit parking lot, empty of cars, forming an unnecessarily large frame around a small yellow convenience store. There was no sign to tell him the name of the store, but a blue and red OPEN sign blinked and winked in its window, illuminating outdated and faded advertisements for cigarettes. The largest depicted an impossibly angular blonde on a field of nauseous yellow, a cigarette between her fingers, shrieking, all her teeth bared. Something in her eyes that caused him tremendous unease. He rushed inside, if only to put the blonde out of his sight. The light was blindingly bright. He angled a hand at his brow and searched the aisles. Behind the rows of chips and jerky and candy he located a bin of nearly frozen sandwiches impaled with toothpicks and smothered in an excess of cellophane. He grabbed one at random. He approached the unmanned counter.

On the television behind the counter, the grinning talk show host held out a long-fingered hand to introduce a magician. Greyson dropped his sandwich and it landed with a small mortal thud. The magician was someone he knew, Haskell, a former apprentice of his, now grown, a young man, baby fat gone. His blonde hair was rolled in a gelled wave; unthinkably, he was clad in faded dungarees and an untucked shirt. He strutted the small stage, pointing out into the unseen crowd, vamping. He exuded confidence. He cocked an eyebrow and pulled pinched fingers up to his ear, slowly extracted a long, gnarled carrot, wincing as it emerged.

Hack! Charlatan!

Haskell placed the carrot on a telephone table, repeated the trick with his other ear. Then he paused. His eyes bugged out and his hand went to his throat, shielding his twitching Adam's-apple. His cheeks puffed out froglike and he affected nausea, dizziness. He staggered, and Greyson found himself staggering a few steps as well, leaning on a display, gaze affixed to the screen. Haskell's stomach contracted, expanded. Then something appeared at his thin, pursed lips. He reached up a tentative hand and pulled. Rabbit ears. He hacked, gagged, stumbled forward.

With a retch, he extracted a small rabbit into his cupped hands.

The rabbit was festooned with strings of saliva; a long line of drool, tinged with bright red blood, wavering slightly in the air, ran from the man's bottom lip to the rabbit's puffed tail. With a sweep of his arm he wiped the saliva away. With his other hand he held the rabbit aloft by the scruff of its neck. The animal looked frightened. The boy placed the rabbit on the table between the two carrots. He raised his arm and turned away from the camera. Tucked into the back of his dungarees was a shining cleaver. He turned back, his face impassive, raised the cleaver in the air.

"All set?" A clerk, thin, a wisp of a mustache, had appeared as though from a trapdoor.

"If by that vague phrase you mean have I been helped, I most certainly have not. If you mean am I ready to transact business, I am... and have been." The clerk sniffed and the two wordlessly, with mutual contempt, exchanged currency for comestibles. Greyson looked back at the television. The blood-spattered talk show set was now teeming with damp rabbits, tethered together by an expansive shivering and glistening web of spittle. The boy magician was fully bent in the center of the set, soaking in the shocked applause. The camera swung over to the host, who was clapping his hands together madly, then to the band leader, who pumped a yellow fist, howling. Horribly, the band leader's bathrobe had fallen open. The clerk, now turned away from Greyson, gaped at the television. He began to applaud, and then to cough, hacking and gasping and clapping his hands. Greyson fled, his right hand fastened over his mouth and nose to prevent the transmission of germs.

He lugged his case to the curb and sat under a streetlight. The wrapping on the sandwich was voluminous and apparently without beginning or end. After considerable effort he was finally able to free the sandwich. It seemed to consist of cold cuts pink and grey between two layers greenish of mayonnaise in which was suspended shreds of lettuce browned at the edges. All of it—bread, meat, and toppings—tasted of old bologna. Greyson stood and tossed the thing into a trash can. He would attempt, perhaps, to sneak an hors d'oeuvre at the venue.

So, his stomach issuing bubbly complaints, he turned from the main thoroughfare and wended his way down narrow avenues with close-together houses, all dark and silent, watched over by crouching cars. He turned onto Tiffany Terrace. At its terminus stood the venue, a tall and profusely turreted mansion that rose high into the starry sky. It was as though the street were nothing more than a long driveway, the other houses mere guard shacks and dormitories for the service staff necessary to maintain a house of that size. The front was lit by spotlights, all the windows ablaze. On a current of air there wafted faint music, a jaunty steam calliope, hissing cymbals, a tuba stalking a muffled trumpet. There were shrieks and laughter and ragged coughing. It sounded like a carnival.

As he lugged his case along, he saw that the other houses on the street appeared to have been abandoned midway through their construction. Their frames leaned right and left; some were partially collapsed onto cross-hatches of warped plywood. Tattered tarpaulins were strewn over piles of bricks and concrete blocks. Further along, there were only foundations, then giant geometric holes in the ground. He fancied he could sense things lurking in those would-be basements, splashing around in rainwater and muck, and he hastened his steps.

He attained the expansive porch, bouncing his case alongside him as he ascended the stone steps. The door was open and he walked into the pink-tiled foyer and looked down both side halls and then into the balcony-lined room ahead. No! It cannot be! Among the guests, mingling, laughing, holding aloft a glass of white wine as he made his way through the crowd—Spettrini! The man was elderly, bent, but he moved like a boy, quick and alive.

Greyson had heard he'd drowned, or been torn apart by a bear... but there he was... or... wait. *Was* it him? Greyson practically sprinted into the room, his case bouncing behind him, only to be accosted by a large man in a powder-blue caftan who slid from a side hallway and blocked Greyson's view. The man's brows and waxed mustache were bright white. "This way," he said. "You're late, you're late."

He put his hand on Greyson's shoulder, grabbed the case with his other hand, and they trotted down a short hall and into a couch-lined side room that ran the length of the house. From the ceiling hung a strange, bulbous chandelier, moist and glowing with reflected light. All about Greyson was a gurgling, rushing sound, as of strong currents of flowing water. As he was hastened along, in an adjacent room he spied Haskell, his former apprentice, apparently fresh from his television appearance. He was seated in an overstuffed easy chair, surrounded by revelers, cradling in his arms a small rabbit whose head lolled loosely—its neck had been broken. Haskell was disconsolate, his mouth slack and his tear-streaked face a shade of red one associates with profound sun-burns. In the next room was the television host, laughing, all gums and teeth, each arm around the waist of a skeletal brunette whose spine jutted from her back like the teeth of serrated knives. Also in that room sat three shivering, wet old women wound tightly in towels, being tended to by paternal, mustachioed sheriffs whose bulging stomachs tested the integrity of their uniforms. And the convenience store kid chatting up a portly blonde in a garish pink pantsuit. And the actor he'd missed on the talk show, waiting for the bathroom, one hand gripping a white handkerchief into which he was gagging loudly, the other grabbing desperately at his crotch in a manner befitting a child.

Finally, Greyson was brought into what he took to be the great room. At its easternmost edge was a vast stage, ringed with chaise lounges, ancient chairs, thrones, couches. From the center of the ovoid chamber, a stone column, thicker than four stout men, rose ceilingward; from it curved great balconies of white marble. Monstrous red curtains obscured the windows; the ceiling was high and far away, a pink and blue blur. But the room was empty of people.

A voice spoke, echoing around the room. *Come back to me*, it said. *I have so much to teach. There are passageways to be conjured, paths to be struck through the walls that confine us to this world.* Into the room through an archway, side-by-side, strode the television host, Haskell, the convenience store clerk, an old woman in a soaked nightgown, and a sheriff. Their clothes melted away as though consumed by invisible fire, and they squeezed together shoulder to shoulder and elongated, horizontal creases forming across their bodies as they became fingers that reached out for Greyson as a section of the column split off and bent to form a great arm. There were blue veins surfacing and pulsing at the narrowing wrist. The arm attached to the fingers, the front-most section flattening into a palm.

As Greyson fled, the walls and ceiling began to vibrate, fluttering like sheets. A terrible shriek tore through the chamber and a figure appeared at the entrance toward which he was heading. It was the woman from the hotel. Freed from her yellow-windowed booth, she was flush with color: rouged cheeks, scarves of brilliant yellow, shining purple, leaf-green. Her scarves rippled as though in a stiff wind. She was ragged, aged, buffeted by time, and absolutely beautiful. "Run," she said. "Get out of this house as fast as your feet can take you." The walls shook and a terrible roar cycled throughout the house like a demon train on an intricate track. A set of white spikes rose from the floor and another sank through the ceiling. They sank into the woman at her neck and up through her left leg. A glut of blood bubbled at her mouth.

Greyson ran. He reached out his hand to touch hers as he passed her. Her skin was warm. There was a jolt, as of static electricity, and as Greyson exited, the chamber began to contract around him. He bounded down the red hall (which was now damp and tinged with purple), reached the porch, bounded to the walk, and ran down the center of the street. The roar was deafening now, the street lit nearly as bright as daylight from behind him. He turned.

White and black hairs were sprouting on the roof of the house, crawling up like a profusion of snakes. The dormer windows went white, and eyeballs, blue and blazing, rolled down into view like window shades. The front door widened, moldings splintering and falling to the ground. It bent into a grin as on either side the half built-houses began to rise like jagged arms, sending clouds of dirt into the air. The road began to split and crumble. Greyson turned again and ran as Spettrini pushed himself out of the ground and the house that was his head ascended into the night sky.

FOLLOWING YOU HOME

Ten minutes before the countdown began, Merrill was depleted. He had worked all day, and only begrudgingly had he let himself be persuaded to forego an evening on the recliner with a blanket and a book, an early bed. He knew only Dave, Myrta and Bellamy, not very well at that, just from work, not even in his department, and they were circulating among the smaller groups, entering and departing conversations with an enviable ease that was alien to Merrill.

The party was within walking distance of his rented house, though, and he could leave at will, at any time, and the weather was mild for the first of the year. But once there, he'd somehow managed his way into a prickly argument in which, unarmed with facts, he rapidly began losing his footing. Dispirited, aggrieved, he wondered at how he might extricate himself, when the countdown began, someone shoved a champagne flute into his hand, all glasses went aloft, and Merrill ducked through the crowd and slid out the door, not before grabbing a malt beverage bottle and three nutmeg logs from a tin.

He buttoned his jacket as he bounced down the hedge-hemmed staircase and into the street, where revelers in puffed-up coats and scarves were dispersing from the city's downtown ceremonies. Shoving the bottle into his pea coat pocket, he kicked at unwound streamers and clumps of confetti dampened with snow. The flurries that had been coming down all afternoon began to turn into a steady snow that covered the city like static.

As Merrill crossed the Main Street intersection he saw, crossing opposite and parallel with him, in a throng of teenagers, what he first thought to be a man in gray carrying a stained, mottled white balloon on a thick string. Looking again, he saw that the balloon was the head of some impossibly tall thing with a deathly pallor and a slender, muscled neck. The crowd around this freakish apparition seemed to not take notice of it at all. Merrill saw nothing of the man's body, and at first thought the thing to be a prank, some kind of outsized macabre puppet surrounded by his handlers, but as the crowd reached the curb, just as Merrill reached the curb opposite, the thing broke away and shambled in his direction. As it passed under the stoplight, Merrill saw the thing's features full on, and his stomach tightened like a fist. It bore no resemblance to any earthly creature he'd ever seen. Everything was…*wrong*. He broke into a jog and at the next crosswalk he bolted back across the street and ducked down an alley that led to a parking lot and a side road. Then he walked between two houses to the long road that led to his house. Turning, he could see the crowds on Main Street and…there it was, that pale head bobbling just below a streetlight, swiveling, searching.

Merrill took a circuitous route home, doubling back, looking behind him frequently and with great apprehension. Across the sky like a rocket shot a keening, a terrible, echoing shriek, like some monstrous cicada, it was a desperate, searing expression of hungry desire, tinged with equal parts outrage and mournfulness. Merrill stopped still, everything inside him clenching now, his teeth pushing against each other. Across the street in a boxy raised ranch he saw two silhouettes appear in a yellow window, black countenances tilted upward toward the sky. Then the light in the room was extinguished, dropping the silhouettes into grey obscurity. The cry reached a searing pitch, then trailed off with sounds like fever-sharp knife edges sliding across one another. The silence that followed was somehow worse, for he knew the cry would sound again, and so it did, not a full minute later, louder and longer this time, causing the muscles in his throat to vibrate, his testicles to pull up into his body for protection, his body shrink itself into a fetal crouch, his hands splaying on the sidewalk like talons.

When it stopped, he ran full-bore to his house, there it was, just ahead, low and blue, the familiar orange glow in the kitchen window. He entered, keys onto telephone table, up to the bathroom where he washed his face and regarded himself momentarily in the mirror. It's okay. It can't find him. He lost it. It was maybe just a man, a deformed man, harmless, celebrating the new year in a city known for tolerating its freaks and its oddballs. Maybe it *had* been a puppet, or...or a hologram...a New Year's prank.

He climbed into his rumpled bed and hit the light. Silence, but for the clicking of the pipes. He pictured that horrific thing, stalking the darkened streets, searching for him. The house creaked, a settling sound, normal. But Merrill's heart jumped, and then beat so hard he wondered if he might have some kind of attack. Did the light change just a touch around the corner from the doorway to the bedroom? Was that a light footstep, tentative, cautious?

Merrill turned on his light and leapt from his bed. He strode about the rooms, chest out, brave of face, turning on all the lights, then to the front door. It looked somehow crouched, poised to burst open and admit unimaginable horror. Strangely, Merrill suddenly felt calm, settled, at a strange ease.

He remembers the bottle in his pocket. He pulls it from his jacket, tossed over the back of a chair, drinks, lemons, sweet and boozy, fizz roiling at the roof of his mouth. The cold from the outside fills the room and turns it icy blue.

He angles the recliner to face the closed door. Considers. Up and opens the door. Sits, facing the staticky rectangle of street and snow-capped hedge, lit by a streetlight. A few leaves skitter by, chasing and teasing each other, relics from a dead and buried autumn.

His eyes blink quickly. More slowly now, more closed than open. He pictures the hideous creature emerging from the thicket like a mantis, gaping black mouth with teeth like a serpent's, dripping with mucousy venom, fingers without bones wriggling with perverse anticipation, eyes deep in fleshy caverns, kaleidoscopic, ruby and rot. Its gnarled torso and limbs are cloaked, he imagines, in blankets that once swaddled bloated and desiccated corpses, sticky with sweat and suppurations, torn and clotted. Its smell is septic, toxic, tinged with a blasphemy of citrus.

And yet, what appears in the doorway, what steps with a long, twig-thin, gnarled white leg, over the transom, what approaches on white, serrated pincers is worse than what he saw on that snow-speckled street, worse than what he had imagined, worse than what he would have been capable of imagining. He greets it with a hoarse, rising shriek of laughter. As it deliberately disrobes him, its horrible head tilted like that of an animal, he gibbers and jabbers and weeps. It plucks his lashes and places them gently, delicately, in his eyes. The pain is unreal. He blinks, rapidly, water filling his eyes. He sees the thing swimming in salt, wavering, leering. Only then does it begin its real cruelties. And after all the monstrous ministrations, all the penetrations and the whisperings, the promises and the betrayals, the lashings, the hoarse imparting, in a nigh-impenetrable accent, of ghastly truths and ghoulish prophecies, it does the worst thing, the cruelest and most horrible act. It leaves Merrill alive.

NO ABIDING PLACE ON EARTH

—Mary, don't forget your cudgel.

Mary mutters, how could she *possibly* forget, grabs the knotted, leaded blackthorn cudgel from the umbrella stand, knocking Daniel's cane to the floor. He shouldn't have said anything, he knew she was in a snit, and of course she knows to bring the cudgel, but...but a father's job is to err on the side of protecting his daughter if he can. And for his trouble, she snaps at him. Mary, little Mary-kins, not so long ago just a doll-faced girl, curious and giggly and adoring, now hardened, weary-eyed, humorless. She slams the door behind her as he pushes himself up from the chair, groaning like a man much older than his 54 years, bends slowly to pick up the cane, stabs it back into the stand. He pulls back the curtain, scans the barren treetops. Their stripped limbs wave in the wind, a skeletal convocation pleading for an offering from the frowning, furrowed sky. Tendrils of mist, the ghosts of snakes, curl around their trunks. The telephone wires bounce gently like recently deserted tight-ropes.

There don't seem to be any of *them* out there, not now.

From the other side of the hedges he hears the car door slam shut, the whinny and purr of the engine. She is okay. She will be okay. The cudgel will be enough.

November, that brown and brittle season, has swung in hard on the heel of Halloween, and most days linger in a dusky malaise from start to finish, suspended in a bluish-grey solution of dread and dead leaves. Last night the wind kicked up hard, barren limbs smacking at the house like dried husks of hands. The windows rattled and shook in their casements and the cat drew close to Daniel in his easy chair, her chin in the crook of Daniel's arm. When the wind yelped around the corners of the house, the cat whimpered, pressing closer. Daniel hoped fervently for the power to stay on.

Most of *them* keep their distance when the lights are on.

It started with the power outages. The first was in mid-September, resolved quickly, unremarkable. Another two days later, lasting nearly three hours. The next week brought four separate outages, over seven hours without electricity each go-round. Flashlights, candles, early to bed. Charge your devices while you can. When in doubt, throw it out.

Another call to MassGrid, a subsidiary of The Global Electricity Group PLC. The unhappy union of squirrel and transformer, said the voice somewhere back in the phone's speaker, distant, like a call from the outer reaches of the universe. *That's what you said every time I called last week. Are the squirrels committing mass suicide?* Silence for a beat, a rote apology. We're sorry sir. Crews are out and active, doing all they can.

Uh huh.

The scratching at the windows starts up. The doorknob jiggles. The muttering, the guttural rumbling, the sighs at the windows, at the doorjamb.

After a time, the house awakens with a hum and the lights flicker bright, too bright, blinding, then back to their usual weak dimness. The things retreat to the trees, beyond the reach of the streetlights.

The outages still come, two or three a day, lasting

hours.

––––––––––

It was early October when Daniel first saw them. He was out for a walk, and he chanced to look up high in the grey sky and one was descending, some kind of strange owl, plucked bare. Pallid, knobby breast; flimsy, webbed wings dangling from twig-like arms, it flew only with a great deal of exertion. When it was a few yards off it began to coast, spreading its wings wide, and lit in a copse of trees, its long-toed feet scrambling to grasp a gnarled branch. Twigs snapped and a flurry of leaves and…and the trees were full of the things. Daniel took a few tentative steps in their direction, then clasped his hand over his mouth. Their heads resembled those of elderly men, wispy white hair, wizened, slack mouths curtained with pink, blistered dewlaps. One turned its hooded, sagging eye in his direction. Then the others did the same. They coughed and wheezed and began flapping their sad wings as if to launch. It sounded like the smacking of slackened cheeks when someone rapidly shakes his head back and forth.

Then they did launch, all of them, at once. Daniel dropped to his knees, covered his head. They swarmed above him, flapping and wheezing and muttering. When they had passed, he turned and saw a boy—the Bernier kid, probably—running down Prospect Street, the horrid flock flying low above him, bellowing and belching and screeching. The front-most creature swooped down and grabbed the boy by the collar and left sleeve of his shirt. He cried out as he was lifted into the sky. The flock ascended into the clouds, the boy struggling to release himself, to punch at the horrid thing that carried him, small legs kicking uselessly at the sky. Daniel stared after them, helpless.

––––––––––

Since *they* came, everything deteriorates with alarming rapidity. The cat litter dampens and clumps into concrete. The milk curdles minutes out of the refrigerator. The bread, fresh from the machine, sprouts green bruises. Peaches erupt with black blisters and crumple, flies bursting from their rotten cores, buzzing madly. Tea cools before it reaches Daniel's lips. He cracks an egg and the yolk is black gelatin. The smell is rank, gag-inducing.

Even the bulbs in the lamps don't have the reach they once did.

The worst thing is that there's nothing about the creatures on the news. Daniel watches the two local channels, scans the daily paper, which the carrier, brave soul, still somehow manages to fling onto the doorstep every day but Sunday. There are three houses on the short dead-end street, three including the one he shares with Mary. The other two have shed their tenants and whatever belongings they could fit in their cars. Daniel wonders where they're going and whether they'll get there. He doesn't know how widespread the problem is. He wishes they'd talk about it on the news.

Mary's been gone four hours, the longest stretch yet. The local markets are locked up tight or else busted open, trashed and looted, and she has to go further and further to find canned food and simple provisions.

Daniel is again left alone with his thoughts. They are not welcome companions. He considers his belly, now hanging over his belt-line. His belt digs into his flesh when he sits, carving painful welts into his waist. His own heartbeat nags him about his mortality. He is aware of it more and more as he ages, especially in the silences when Mary's gone out or sits sequestered in her room. It thumps out the years like a kitchen timer. Like anything else, it will stop, ring the harsh and jarring bell of finality. It could do so at any moment, as his father's had; the old man had simply crumpled to the kitchen floor while scrambling eggs, the spatula gripped in his white-knuckled hand.

Further, Mary has been complaining that she can hear his snoring from her room. He probably has sleep apnea. Stops breathing who knows how many times a night. And he speculates at what tiny cancers might even now be multiplying somewhere in the murky purple depths of his body. He turns over in his tired mind every fatal scenario he can conjure. Death flies among his thoughts, a black wraith tracing a zig-zag path among moon-drunk birds.

Daniel turns on the television to silence his thoughts. Channel 22 is interviewing a beloved coach about his retirement...and damned if one of the things isn't perched atop city hall in the background, blurry, but unmistakable; its spindly legs twitching; rheumy, hate-filled eyes surveying the town common. Daniel sits up in the chair, stares. His hands open and close. He wants to shout, to warn the people on the screen. The thing's talons scrape the brick, red clouds spill down onto the walk below. A couple walking below see the thing, flinch, scurry into traffic, protecting their faces with crossed forearms among the screaming of car brakes and the shouts of horns. Not a word from the reporter as the coach prattles on, oblivious. The thing launches awkwardly from its perch, lurches through the sky and off-screen.

He calls the station's You Report It Hotline. The phone rings and rings.

The door slams and the cat bolts from Daniel's lap and runs into the kitchen. Mary rushes in and the hood of her coat is torn, her forehead scraped, dots of blood clotting along a ragged line like points on a graph. Her strawberry blonde curls are matted, mud-caked. Daniel starts to rise and she flutters a dismissive hand in his direction.

-*Fucking things. I'm fine. Where's the disinfectant...I've got it.*

Off to the bathroom. The sink runs, water splashes. A door closes and music starts up and she's in her room ignoring everything. She has been stoic, sullen since before this thing began, since the disaster with Keith, about which she refused to give any information at all—an incident, Daniel supposed, or an unresolved argument—that saw her arrive at Daniel's unannounced with a suitcase full of clothes and unknown depths of unexpressed rage and disappointment. Now he is unwillingly cast in the role of the father who can't do or say anything right, and all he can do is wait for her to come around. It would feel better, he thinks, to have an ally. It would feel better for her too, he knows it. Until she comes around, the feline will more than suffice for uncomplicated companionship. As though summoned by the thought, the cat saunters back into the room, tail swimming lazily behind her. She jumps to Daniel's side and sinks into sleep.

That night, something new, something bad. Daniel awakens to voices echoing outside, unintelligible, punctuated with dark chortling and sibilant whispers. He feels for the cat but she is no longer at his side. He rises, crosses the dark room to the window, parts the curtain. The moon is high and bright, the sky cloudless. Stars glint, smug and safe up in the firmament. The emptied houses' windows hang open, and the voices thrum within, in the dark, empty rooms. He can't make out individual words, can't even tell if they're speaking English. The voices overlap, converge and declaim in unison, then part into separate streams of droning monologues. They don't stop for breaths. Daniel turns on the fan to block out the sounds with white noise, but still he hears the percussive voices, now strident, now clandestine, now ecstatic. He falls into uneasy sleep as the cat, who has returned to his side, twitches and squeaks out complaints, her tiny teeth clicking.

In the morning Daniel dares step out onto the porch, then down to the lawn. It's warm for November. The sun glistens off the dewy branches that crowd the quiet street. He hears birdsong, a rare sound now. They sound cautious, staccato chirps and trills and titters. The windows of the other houses are still open, but all is still. He doesn't even see any of them. He usually sees two or three sleeping at dawn, tucked into the crook of a branch or on a housetop. They clench like wounded spiders, and they shiver and twitch. Their ribs stick out. Their sides heave. One will, on occasion, push out a loud, rattling fart. Daniel once saw one break wind, wake, and, grotesque arms pinwheeling, fall from its perch on a high telephone wire. He laughed— he could not help but laugh—but he stopped laughing when it hit the ground. He has to block his memory now of what happened when it hit the ground.

Beyond the hedge he spots Mary's shoe on the road and his heart starts to thrum in his chest. The air seems to buzz with menace. Dark droplets on the pavement lead to the shoe, or away from it. Are they blood drops? He backs up, keeping an eye on the space between the hedges. He closes the door and latches it, heads for Mary's room. The door is open, the bed unmade, the sheets and blankets piled at its foot.

He goes back outside, grabs his cane on the way out. A flimsy weapon, but a weapon nonetheless. The cat yowls as he passes. The shoe is still there, and now he hears something. A whimper. Holding the cane out in front of him in both hands, he advances toward the street. He braces himself, passes between the hedges. He looks at the shoe, kneels, touches a droplet and examines the tip of his finger. Brown liquid has settled into the whorls of his fingertips. He sniffs at it, wincing. Not blood. Motor oil.

Mary's car is still in its spot. He rises and turns to go back inside.

Three of them stand sentry in front of the front door. They are emaciated. Blue veins as thick as fingers pulse in their sagging wings. The layered, drooping folds under their eyes are black and bruised. One has a skin tag the size of an apple hanging on its cheek, dark red and bleeding at its root. Its weight pulls down the skin under its eye, creating a cradle of red below the pupil in which maggots cavort in a squirming orgy. The things open their mouths, revealing purple-soiled graveyards of disarranged grey teeth, and sing a high, mournful chorus, an alien, synchronized sigh. A barbershop quartet, Daniel thinks. But where is the fourth?

Hot, damp hands grasp the back of his neck and squeeze.

The thing whips him around, dropping him onto his back and pinning him, its wings flapping wildly. Daniel's cane flies from his hand, landing in the hedge. The thing's feet dig into his gut below the arch of his rib cage. Its eyes betray fierce anger rimmed around the edges with profound sorrow. It pulls Daniel's face to its own—Daniel deliberately unfocuses his eyes and lets his mouth go slack—and it kisses him gently on the lips, dry and feathery.

It loosens its grip and rolls off of Daniel onto the leaf-strewn walk. Its hands grapple uselessly at the air and it coughs, its body trembling with each concussive hack. Then the trembling quickens, its toes spread and stretch, and it dies, its eyes rolled rightward, staring through Daniel and into unknown abysses. It clenches and shoots a stream of miserable grey diarrhea onto the walk.

Daniel pushes himself into a sitting position, lurches forward, and stands. His legs are weak and shaking. The veins stand out in his arms as he puts his hand to the back of his neck to check for blood. It stings. It stings like a thousand jellyfish. The three things that had been blocking the door have flown up to the eaves, where they weep noisily, shining pendulums of yellow-green mucous swaying from their nostrils.

Daniel retrieves his cane, makes his way up the porch steps, caroms through the front doorway and into the dark living room, falls into his easy chair. He closes his eyes, listens to his own breathing as it calms. At some point the cat jumps onto the arm of the chair, then jumps back down and gallops out of the room hissing. His skin feels as though it's shrinking, tightening in increments like a blood pressure cuff. His arms feel week and flabby. He tries to lift one and cannot. His eyes burn and he is unable to attend to them. *Am I dying?* he wonders. *Am I dead?*

The answer comes two hours later when the creak of the door awakens him. He lifts the lid of one eye and sees Mary silhouetted in the evening light. She smells of blood, of infected flesh. Oh, Dad, she says, and she comes and kneels next to him. She touches his face with one hand, lifts his wrist with the other. Her hands are as hot as fire.

Oh my god, Dad, she says.

KUKLALAR

Artemis entered without knocking and rapped his knuckles on the side of the filing cabinet. I was struggling with the wording of an Official Company Statement due to my superiors before the end of the day, so I shook my head no, but he held up three fingers, each meant to represent one minute of my time. I rolled back my chair, stood, and pulled on my jacket. I knew from experience that it would take considerably longer than advertised, and I'd already guessed the topic of the desired conversation: the renovations, now in their third week, smirking workmen and ladders and dust, wires hanging from the drop ceiling like intestinal loops, no word from corporate as to what exactly was being installed. Impeding one's progress through the corridors were ladders, unruly deadfalls of metal tracks, large metal tool cases, and industrial-size rolls of high-tensile wire that resembled metallic hay bales, materials for the installation of two sets of tracks into the hallway ceilings and the running of wires along them. The noise proved intrusive and distracting: drilling, hammering, sawing, instructions shouted from man to man.

In fact, Artemis did not want to talk about that. We stood with our backs to the wall in the courtyard between the two buildings that comprised the campus, shielded from the rain by a slight overhang. He ran his hands back and forth over his rumpled white hair until his coiffure came undone, forming a storm cloud around his head. He looked like a mad scientist. Shielding his lighter from the wind, he lit a cigarette, and I lit my own off of his. His ruddy hand trembled as he drew the smoke into his lungs. I noted the dry skin at his knuckles, honeycombed with cracks, some of them red with blood. "There's a cabal against me in this place," he said, smoke billowing out around the words.

"Do you think so?" I said.

"Martina Denton's in on it. And Glen what's-his-name. Dale Kherr, in Maintenance? What it *is* is, the people in power don't like me because I lack an internal censor—I got this from my father, who was fired from more jobs than I've ever held—I tell them the truth. The *unadorned* truth." He pointed a cigarette-yellowed finger at me and jabbed it into the air a few times. "And do I like being in this situation? Do I enjoy being on the bubble?"

"Of course not."

He grinned, revealing teeth stained from tobacco smoke and profusely chipped at the edges. "Of *course* not. It's just that I'm not...what's the word?"

"Constitutionally."

"Not consti*tuti*onally able to prevent myself doing so." He paused, looked skyward. "I think I was looking for 'congenitally.' At any rate, I want you to watch my back, will you? If you hear anything, anything they might have on me, you'll let me know, won't you, buddy? Can I give you that assignment? Will you be my eyes and ears, if I keep it at that, anatomically speaking?"

I said that I would.

Again with the jabbing finger. The nail in need of trimming, a brown line at the distal edge. His grin was manic; an odd light danced in his eyes. "Don't shit in my hat and tell me it'll fit better."

I confirmed that I would not.

We finished our cigarettes and thumbed the butts into the receptacle. As we walked back to the building, two of the young women from customer service passed us, fishing packs of cigarettes from their purses. Artemis turned around to look. "Oh man," he said. "Oh man."

I worried about Artemis. His conflicts with management had grown more frequent over the course of several years, and he worked himself up into a rage at the merest perceived insult. I suspected that actual slights were in fact very rare, or at the very least harmless, or meant in jest. I feared that one day he would step over some line, or simply provoke the wrong person. What would become of him if he were fired? He was nearing 60, and the skills he brought to bear at A.I.I. did not translate well in the larger corporate world; moreover, the confidentiality agreement that he—that all of us—had signed was stringent and strict and carried outsized professional and personal penalties for those who might violate it.

However, the man did wield incredible intellectual prowess; that I knew just from conversations over lunch and smoke breaks. When he was not preoccupied with cabals and conspiracies, he spoke at length about films from countries I'd never heard of, classical music, the writings of the great philosophers. Of late he'd become obsessed with the works of long-dead mystics and occultists, Crowley and Blavatsky and Geist and the like, and he spoke about them with almost childlike enthusiasm.

Man could, he insisted, and here I paraphrase to the point of possibly profound distortion—affect with his mind the world around him, not only plant life and weather systems, but sentient creatures. The more advanced man, the more *studied* man might even be able to affect the minds of other men—something far beyond the hypnosis propagated by hucksters and hacks. Maybe, he said, even inanimate objects. It was nothing as prosaic as telekinesis. It involved uttered sounds and elixirs and energies released into the "mindscape of the psychic environment"…man could, if he had the access to certain secret knowledge, imbue the very cells of things and beings around him with his will. Sometimes he would pull out a pen and draw formulae—three-dimensional equations of dizzying complexity, or else utter nonsense— on a restaurant napkin. I confess that most of what he said lay well beyond my capacity to understand it, and I would go to bed those nights with my neck aching from an abundance of polite nodding. He either did not notice or generously chose to ignore the fact that I would contribute virtually nothing to these discussions.

In contrast to Artemis, who liked to talk back, to spar, sometimes even without any intent beyond entertaining himself, my custom for the eight or so hours that constituted each workday consisted largely of going unnoticed as much as possible. I did the work that was assigned to me, and if I asked a question, it was not to challenge nor contradict, but to request information that might inform my tasks, or allow me to perform them more efficiently. If asked to do an unpleasant task, I assented cheerfully, and as a result my work existence was free of difficulty and of dramatics. Those I experienced vicariously through Artemis. I admit to having found some perverse entertainment in his paranoid fantasies.

What I couldn't understand, though, was his leering after the young girls in the office. They were unformed, not yet fully come into being. They were a sculptor's unfinished thing. They held no interest for me. To be fair, though, my libido had long been on some kind of downslide. It worried me, but only academically. Practically, the lack of that intense, cumbersome drive improved life both at work and outside of the office.

Not long after the ceiling work had begun, a separate group of workmen in blue jumpsuits arrived in a long white van, carrying with them duffle bags the approximate length of caskets. Workmen hustled them in pairs. Each had two vinyl handles and some inscrutable design sewn in with thread the color of Giallo movie blood. The workmen stacked the bags in the glass-walled conference room adjacent to the main hall over the course of an hour. Once they were all in, the workmen drew the shades, darkening the hall and piquing the curiosity of the staff, who gathered in clusters in the cafeteria to exchange theories and express frustration at the company's culture of secrecy.

The next day I planned to phone in to the office to beg off work for the day. I had been experiencing a mental fatigue whose symptoms were a pointed disinterest in completing the tasks I'd scheduled for the day, along with a general aversion to communicating in any medium with colleagues and clients and press. But before I could make the call, an email alert came through on my phone. In order to complete the construction, it read, the office would be closed Thursday, Friday, and Monday, and business would resume Tuesday morning.

Tuesday came too soon. I shuffled in that morning to discover that the workers had extended the tracks from the halls into the offices, laboratories, cubicles, kitchens, meeting rooms, and stairwells. Mercifully, they did not extend into the lavatories. In all of our inboxes was an email. Finally they would reveal the purpose of the construction. I opened it and read.

As part of AII's efforts to restructure and to focus our energies more fully on our work, we have taken the step of eliminating many of our middle management positions. Supervisory roles will now be filled remotely from our central office in Leeds, Massachusetts. Twelve men selected by Wren Black himself will fill these roles on our three east coast campuses. The supervisors will be represented here by the Kuklalar. *The invention of Cordvassant Machines, the* Kuklalar *are humanoid marionettes, equipped with cameras and microphones. They will be present for your day-to-day activities. At least one will be present at every meeting. They will be the eyes and ears of Annelid Industries International.*

The Kuklalar *are not equipped for audio and will remain mute. It is not their job to interact, nor to tutor nor teach. They will not speak. On Monday morning of each week, your supervisor, represented by a* Kuklala, *will prepare a list of tasks and goals for the week ahead. At the end of the day, your supervisor will prepare a one-page report summarizing and analyzing your activities, followed by a weekly summary report on Friday afternoon. We invite you to join us in the atrium at* 11:00 *a.m. for an official introduction to our new supervisory staff. We expect that you'll welcome them and afford them every courtesy.*

Sure enough, the desk of my previous supervisor, Dan Wojick, had been emptied of his papers and personal effects. This was not a tremendous loss. Dan had harbored a childlike enthusiasm for goal-setting, for efficacy, and for "accountability" (my least favorite, for it presupposed wrongdoing of some kind), and he favored a kind of corporate-speak that chafed me. He'd insisted on weekly "check-in" meetings, which cut into time I needed to complete my tasks and which were quite useless, as he would do the bulk of the talking, staring almost cross-eyed at the little notebook he used to record God knows what, while I strained to not glance the wall clock behind him. He was otherwise genial, but the company had been right to eliminate his position—he was of little use.

The Facilities department had packed the atrium full. They'd set up three rows of black-cushioned chairs on either side of the hall, as well as a row along the walkway above. Ten minutes before the spectacle was to begin, the seats had all been taken. As more staff arrived, they took their places behind the rows of chairs, or else stood on the staircase, occasionally shifting to clear a path for a latecomer. I had arrived early and claimed one of the seats in the front. It is advantageous to be seen as taking an interest.

At precisely 11:00 a.m., spotlights along the underside of the walkway lit up and swooped over to illuminate two large metal panels in the ceiling. The Human Resources director, an unsmiling white-shirted stick figure named Blaughmann, lurched in from the reception area to a smattering of applause. He adjusted the mic at his collar and cleared his throat. The amplification of the sound caused some to chuckle. I spotted Artemis across the way, three rows in. His head swiveled left and right, eyes searching, mouth set in a scowl. I raised a hand to try to catch his attention, but he looked everywhere except in my direction.

"Ladies and gentlemen," said Blaughmann, "I know you are as eager as I am to greet our new management team. A lot of people worked very diligently to bring them to you, so I would like to thank Cordvassant Machines for their collaboration, and the facilities team for getting us set up. I would also like to thank you for your patience over these last weeks. I'm aware of the inconvenience it caused, and proud to see how you did not let it affect the high quality of your work. Without further ado, I present to you the *Kuklalar*."

The panels in the ceiling opened like elevator doors, and a thin humanoid figure slowly descended to the floor along a thin wire. *My god*, I remember thinking. *It looks like a lynching*. The figure was made entirely of painted and lacquered wood, down to the brown business suit, white Arrow shirt, and red necktie. Its hair was painted brown with thin grooves carved in to simulate texture, parted on the right. Its chin was on its chest. It landed on its feet, knees bending slightly, and the spotlight swooped down to frame the scene. The *Kuklala* crouched like a ballerina, knees apart, head down, one wooden hand splayed on the carpet. The wire retracted into the ceiling.

Then the *Kuklala* sprang upright with a flourish, both arms in the air. Its features resembled those of a department store mannequin, thin nose, cheekbones high and haughty, the eyes sightless marbles with a faint blue glow. As the gathered crowd applauded, the *Kuklala* looked about the room as behind it, five more descended, landed, mimicked the actions of the first.

They walked up and down the hall, regarding the crowd as the crowd regarded them. They were meant, I think, to appear as visiting dignitaries, or Special Guests. To me they looked rather like drill sergeants. Maybe it was because their wooden hands were clasped behind their backs, their chins upturned. They looked like they had already begun judging us and had found us wanting.

―――――――――――――

The attitude around the office, at least among the men, toward the *Kuklalar* started off as an uneasy mix of humor and general resentment. They ridiculed the *Kuklalar*, and that ridicule was thickly laced with loathing. One afternoon I saw Stanfort, whose office was next door to mine, walking behind one of them, thrusting his hips and pumping his fists. Not long after, I heard, he got two warnings: one for insubordination and one for having violated the company's sexual harassment policy. The women viewed the *Kuklalar* without humor; among them there was much talk about circulating a petition, claiming that the *Kuklalar* had leering eyes, and were given to vague but disquieting gesticulations. It was also noted with much gravity that there were no female *Kuklalar*.

For two weeks, the *Kuklala* who had been appointed to supervise me, whose name tag read "Tombaugh", stood behind me and watched me work. I've a strong aversion to having anyone look over my shoulder, but the thing stood so damned still, I began to think of it more as furniture. Only once did it try to follow me to the restroom, and I informed it of my intention, and it spun around and resumed its place behind my chair. Its end-of-week reports were reserved but neutral, its "analyses" obvious and shallow.

Artemis was having a tougher time of things. "Roundhill is a little martinet," he said, one Monday morning out at the smoking area. "It countermands me. It nitpicks my work. Its reports are *totally* unfair. Clearly someone has informed the home office exactly what they think of me. I can't take it, man. One day I'm going to bring Roundhill right to the paper-cutter."

He didn't do exactly that, but what he did cost him his livelihood.

I heard the calamity before I saw it. There were shrieks and someone--I think it was Shelly in Accounts Receivable—yelling "Water! Get water!" I pushed myself up out of my chair and stepped into the hallway, only to have to immediately duck back in. One of the Kuklalar, engulfed in roaring flames, was zipping down the hall toward the atrium. The thing emitted a terrible ceaseless squeal, a sound like amplified feedback. The knee of its left leg had locked, the tip of its shoe dragging along the carpet behind it; while the right leg mimicked the action of running. I later discovered that my eyelashes had been singed as I pulled back from the conflagration. After it passed, I stepped back out again, only to narrowly avoid a collision with Ollie, the I.T. supervisor, who was barreling after the thing. I followed.

When I reached the atrium, the singed remains of the Kuklala were ascending into the ceiling. The panels closed and a grey cloud spilled down into the hallway. I covered my mouth and nose with my tie. After a beat or two the panels reopened and the Kuklala, just a smoking, blackened thing, spilled to the floor. As the maintenance men were detaching it from the wire, I looked up to see two security men strong-arming Artemis down the stairs.

"Gregor," Artemis was shouting. "We were *friends*! How can you rough-handle me like this? Where do you get the right? Are you that much of a company man?" He looked at me. "Stop this," he said. "Don't let them do this to me."

"I'm sorry," I said. I meant it. It was truly an unfortunate set of circumstances.

It was a week later to the day when everything went to hell. The summer storm that had been predicted had swelled to a hurricane, and meteorologists fell over themselves to predict the worst. You could hear in their voices the sincere hope for a swarm of tornadoes. Management had requested a skeleton crew to remain in the office to keep systems running and to activate a series of protocols put in place in the event of a power failure. I volunteered. The offered overtime pay would afford me some much-desired financial buffer. I brought with me a folding cot, a change of clothes, a paperback book, and two days' worth of canned meals. It was me, Dale from maintenance, Glen from I.T., and Martina from Receiving. For the first hour or so, all was still, and we began to speculate that the storm had been simply a matter of hype and hyperbole and predicting the worst in the face of a variety of weather models. The overtime pay was worth it, all agreed. We split up and went to our respective work spaces.

I was two chapters deep into the book I'd brought when the wind kicked up hard, whistling around the corners. I heard the roar of torrential rain, and then a slam of thunder…and the lights went out.

I tried to call Glenn's extension, and then Martina's, but the phone lines must have been affected by the storm. The emergency lights hadn't come on, which means the backup generators hadn't activated—and that system had been advertised as being able to withstand even the most savage of winds. Without it, we couldn't protect our systems, couldn't preserve nor protect our data nor the specimens in our labs. I activated the flashlight on my cellphone and headed down the hall to meet the others at the atrium—it seemed to me the natural spot to convene and to try to determine where the failure was. I shone my flashlight on the floor in front of me as I went.

About halfway there, I heard over the whistling of the wind a faint noise like blinds being drawn. The sound increased in volume and I raised the flashlight and peered into the gloom. A pale oval emerged from the darkness, morphed into a face. Then out of the blackness sailed one of the *Kuklalar*. Its head had sprung from its neck and bounced gently atop a thick metal coil through which ran wires red, blue and black. It stared at me crookedly with one eye; the other lolled low, as though monitoring the condition of the carpet. Its arm raised slightly as it passed, as if to touch me, and I pressed myself against the wall, barely avoiding contact. It turned right into the darkness of one of the conference rooms, and I heard a slurred and low voice mumble something I could not quite make out, and then utter a shrieking cackle.

I hurried in the opposite direction, toward the atrium, the glow from the flashlight bouncing before me. When I arrived, I saw that a *Kuklala* had pushed Dale up against the wall. Its mouth was at Dale's ear, and it was shoving at him with its hands. Dale bellowed NO, NO, NO, like he was trying to communicate with some rabid animal, and elbowing the thing to no avail. I grabbed it by its shoulder pads and flung it to the ground. Dale collapsed onto his stomach, then rolled onto his back. His face was very pale and his eyes were unfocused. Then they did focus—he was looking beyond me, and his face betrayed a hopeless terror.

I turned. The *Kuklala*'s stomach had swelled, burst from its shirt. Red fault lines spread along its surface until finally it split wide, spilling an abundance of what appeared to be wooden marbles out onto the carpet. I picked one up and instantly threw it back to the floor with a shout. It was slick to the touch, wet with a foul smelling oil of some kind. It smelled like maggoty garbage, like gangrene and spoiled meat. I gagged helplessly. Dale shrieked. The marbles had begun to unfurl, little legs and arms pulling away from the bodies, little faces, dead faces. I clambered to my feet as they swarmed over him. They tore at his flesh and spit it away. To this day I have never heard a sound such as the one Dale was making, from man nor animal, nor do I wish to ever again.

Another *Kuklala* sprung from the shadows. Expansive black wings unfolded at its back. Its eyes went black and its mouth expanded and opened, great tusk-like fangs sprouting from the wooden gums. Its hands turned to talons and then its feet did as well, the shoes growing fault lines, splitting, falling to the ground. It rose toward the ceiling like some great ascending demon, then swooped down onto Martina. It grabbed her by her shoulders and pulled her up toward the skylights. Its legs began to kick at her the way a kitten kicks a toy, shredding her lower back. Tattered clothing and skin fell among the rain of blood into the atrium.

I fled into the storm. The wind and rain lashed me, whipped at my clothing. I got into my car and caught my breath. I closed my eyes. I wondered whether I should go back in, whether I should call the Employee Service Hotline. At that thought I had to laugh. Some kid making twelve dollars an hour. What would I tell him? I opened my eyes, and saw a *Kuklala* approaching my car. It was about ten yards away. It had shed its clothing. Wooden nipples dotted its chest, and awful prosthetic genitalia bounced grotesquely as it approached. Its mouth was a gaping maw, blacker than the storm clouds above. Its eyes glowed a fierce blue. I put the car in reverse, keeping my eyes locked on its eyes. I hit the gas hard and backed out of the lot, backed down the access road until its eyes were small specks smeared by the rain on the windshield. Then I put the car in drive, spun it around, and drove straight to Artemis's house.

Laurel Woods had begun as a sylvan spiritual or religious community in the mid-1700s; the exact nature of the faith lost to time. It started as not much more than a cluster of cabins around a central meeting area, where ancient trees had been sheared away, their stumps fashioned into crude seats facing a massive oak cut into an altar. The community lasted well into the 1980s, cabins morphing into houses, the meeting area growing a ceilinged and plant-strewn pergola, until one November day the residents vanished. It was not the sort of case where food was left cooking, televisions blaring at empty rooms, books laid unfinished in unmade beds; no, the houses were emptied to the bare walls, rooms swept, fixtures and sinks immaculately cleaned. After some push-and-pull between the banks and the city, developers swarmed in. Thus commenced renovations and updates and inspections and assessments, and after a time the houses were put up for sale. They were considerably cheaper (and considerably smaller) than the houses closer to the city center, but they were solid and well-built, and after a series of well-attended community open-houses, they did not sit on the market for long.

Artemis lived in Laurel Woods in a post-modern looking little house shaped like an angled tower; its north-facing wall mostly glass. The considerable foliage kept the sun out; otherwise for several long hours a day the glare would be unconducive to habitation. The living space consisted of three stories connected by a spiral staircase. Except for the ground floor kitchen and bathroom, each story consisted of only one room. The second floor housed the living room; the topmost the bedroom, smallish due to the angled ceiling and the abbreviation by a walled-off crawlspace for storage, accessible by a half-door. Artemis had invited me over for dinner on two or three occasions after I'd started work at A.I.I. Decoration was not among his strong suits. The walls remained bare; the furniture a hodgepodge of Salvation Army couches and armchairs and tables, some ancient and hardy; others fashioned from chipped particle board. Books stood in askew towers along the walls of the living room. An old boxy television dozed atop a slightly bowed, faded red milk crate whose interstices were topped with a layer of dust; I'd wondered whether the thing even worked. The whole of the house was lit with crookedly screwed together halogen floor lamps. Cobwebs fluttered in the corners at the ceiling.

As I approached Laurel Woods, I could see light blazing from all the windows in Artemis's house; it threw shadow-strewn light into the treetops. I pulled up behind his silver Mercury Sable, and I saw that his front door stood open, spilling light onto the walk. I got out of my car, headed up the walk, and entered. No one was in the kitchen, but sounds emanated from up the stairs; I heard a woman titter with laughter, heard someone hush her. "Artemis?" I called. "I'm coming up." My voice sounded foolish to me, cracked and almost hysterical.

I had ascended about halfway up the staircase when a shadow fell over me. Artemis was looking down at me. His hair was wild, his grin wilder, his eyes wilder still. "I wondered if you'd come," he said. His voice sounded odd, the way one sounds after several injections of Novocain, or, further, with a dentists' tools invading the cave of his mouth. The lower part of his face had swollen slightly, his jowls and cheeks flushed red.

I just stared, my hand gripping the railing. "Come up," he said, backing up and out of my range of vision. "Come up and see."

When I attained the landing, I saw the two young women from work sitting cross-legged on the sagging couch. They were naked, covering their torsos with perspiration-browned pillows. Their faces were as red as rust. I felt myself redden too. Behind the couch stood Artemis, clad only in a faded blue bathrobe. His hands sat on the bare shoulder of each woman. Splayed out before the women on the low coffee table were parts of a disassembled *Kuklala*. Its bulbous genitalia were stuffed into a beer mug, lolling in a yellow-orange liquid. Its head sat on its side, the face painted over with a terrible screaming visage, all smeared lipstick and blackened eyes. Severed bird wings and wooden marbles were scattered across the table, and incense cones sent ceilingward fecal brown ribbons, like smokestacks in a surreal city. The incense reeked with a sharp smell I could not identify. Books lay open between the women on the couch, old books, frayed fingers of string reaching from their tattered spines. The smell of the ancient paper merged with the odor of the incense, and I felt a pulse of nausea in my belly.

The room swelled, the walls bulging outward, the lights intensifying. The ceiling lifted and the floor sagged like a tarp over hot gelatin. I struggled to maintain my footing. Artemis laughed. So did the girls. Then they flung away their pillows; in slow motion they sailed through the air.

"There was a price," the girls said in unison, their voices husky and low. "There is always a price." Artemis's lips moved in time with their words.

Artemis opened his mouth and draped his fattened tongue down over his chin. Planted in the tongue was an eyeball, a black horizontal pupil ringed in green-brown. The red, bruised edges of his tongue closed over it like eyelids and opened again, a vertical white inner eyelid briefly visible as it opened like a sliding door.

"He's seen inside us," said the girls, mouthed Artemis. "Deep…deep…"

Artemis let his bathrobe fall to the floor. He approached me, somehow able to maintain his balance on the undulating floor, his hands grasping, three eyes burning.

I was fired from A.I.I. by telephone for dereliction of duty. Staff had to be flown in to recover lost data; the last

I heard, seventy percent or so had been recovered. The lab losses were unrecoverable. The cost, they said, depleted whatever severance to which I might otherwise have been entitled. I have enough savings to get me by for a month, maybe a few weeks beyond that if I am uncharacteristically frugal. I have a retirement fund from which I might borrow, with considerable penalties.

I do not mind. Even with my newly acquired disabilities, I am still eminently hirable. I have experience with terrible things, with unspeakably cruel ecstasies. The vagaries and challenges of the workaday world will offer the banality I need. The tracks that hang over me; the wires from which I depend: I trust that they will guide me.

THE STAY-AWAKE MEN

*W*hat is *radio, exactly?*
I've worked in radio for most of my adult life,
and I can spit out a bunch of words like
electromagnetic energy *and* transmitter *and* antennae. *I*
can talk of frequencies *and* wavelengths *and* circuits… *but*
ultimately I don't understand what the hell I'm talking
about. Even when I look at diagrams that claim to present a
visual representation, my mind just sort of blanks out, hits a
wall, like when I try to imagine an infinite space.

Ultimately—and it pains me to admit this, because I am
a realist, and a reasonably smart man who puts no stock in
the notion of ghosts or gods—I don't believe in the so-called
science.

Because radio is nothing less than magic. Black magic,
because it seems somehow wrong, something that should be
forbidden, and because it is a perverse thrill to sit here in
this studio the size of a broom closet, where the HVAC is
third-rate and the chairs are uncomfortable and the carpet
is peeling up from the floor, and my voice can reach you in
your car, your living room, in your secret space. To you, the
listener, I could be in a palace, in a mansion, astride a
satellite orbiting the earth…anywhere.

And I could say anything. Anything at all.

When people ask me how radio works, I say that we are
tinkering with the empty spaces in the world. That it's just
another kind of pollution, the ramifications of which we

don't yet know. It's as good an explanation as any.

What do I like about radio? What grips me, keeps me tuning in, captivates me more than books and television and movies?

The voice.

The voice is all-important.

Compression, effects, amplification.

Keep your mouth three-to-five inches from the mic. Never trail off at the end of a sentence. Enunciate. Eliminate "umms" and "uhs" from your speech.

Compression, effects, amplification.

The voice you hear is not the voice of the man who is speaking, of the announcer, whoever he is. The voice itself is artifice, and I believe that casts the content into doubt. They enter through your ears and rummage around in your brain, like some kind of terrible insect, devouring, devastating…transforming.

You turn the knob, hear the click, and the voice fills up the room, almost as liquid fills the vessel into which it's poured.

You, the listener, have allowed the announcer in, invited the vampire over the threshold and into your secret space. The announcer, whoever he is, vampire, leech, holds sway now.

The announcer is more powerful than words on a page, than a face speaking from a screen. Because you can close your eyes. Close your eyes. Close your eyes.

The station wagon leaned like a derelict under an insect-dimmed streetlight on the road's shoulder, the passenger side tires off the edge of the pavement and in the gravel. Inside, Don Wright shined a flashlight onto an unfolded map. On the passenger seat next to him, atop a pile of crumpled fast food bags and unopened mail, lay a torn sheet of paper with driving directions he'd scrawled in pencil hours earlier, now slightly smeared and mostly illegible.

Don knew the center of the city well, having been raised among its skyscrapers and smokestacks, its storefronts and bus stops, its parks and plazas. But the outskirts—with their endless shrub lined streets, dingy shops, and sagging houses—were like those of some distant, neglected city. Whenever he drove through unfamiliar neighborhoods such as these, he was struck by the sheer number of people in the city…in the country. In the *world*. Apartment house after apartment house after apartment house, and more around every corner, snaking off down hills, around curves, out of view, but there, endlessly there, crowding him, squeezing him in until his shoulders were up at his ears.

Until he'd passed beyond the familiar grid and into the outskirts, the ride had been easy. He'd sailed through all the red lights—a dozen or more—unassailed, the cars behind him following his lead. There hadn't been as much as the admonishing honk of a car horn. But now he'd had to double back twice, having found himself at the end of unmarked dead-end streets and different roads with the same exact names, and he feared he might be late. The thought soured his stomach. He'd been brought up to arrive ten minutes early at the very latest, one of the rare parental tenets against which he'd never felt inclined to rebel. Show up early or don't show up at all.

It seemed unlikely to Don that any movie studio, even the shadiest, even XT100, would hold a screening in the ugly cluster of warehouses out here beyond the ragged underbelly of the Interstate. He'd have figured the Civic Center, or maybe the sprawling Cineplex on the side of the city closest to Charlton, a sprawling, affluent suburb. But the email—from donotreply@XT.bss.org—had provided only the obscure address and a semi-literate "official" invitation. A few days later Don discovered in his mailbox among the credit card come-ons and the catalogs and the FINAL NOTICES an unmarked, unstamped packet of promotional materials. This consisted mainly of lobby cards, poster postcards, and clippings of advance reviews that revealed frustratingly little about the content of the movie. Also included was a one-page biographical sketch about the movie's subject, and a two-page folded booklet that dealt with the attendant rumors and legends.

Don, having been involved in broadcasting for most of his adult life, had known a little bit of the story, passed around from jockey to anchorman, producer to sound engineer. But sitting in his kitchen a week or so back, a cigarette shrinking slowly in an amber glass ashtray before him, he found himself hungry to know more, to know everything, about the man who had wandered off and became a legend, a myth, a spook story.

The biographical details were sketchy at best. Alan Rampart. Thirty-one years old. Shy and kind and quick to smile, but not given much to laughter. Family man with a son and a daughter. Dragged the family from city to city spinning top forty shlock, earning a pittance. Comes alive at the mic, becomes a different man altogether. Spewing that DJ blather without pause, talking right up to the start of the vocal—*hitting the post* was the term. Appearances at state fairs, announcing the opening acts and the headliners at big rock shows (always, always, you get booed at the big rock shows), at car dealerships, and at purportedly booze-free high school dances. Rumors of cocaine abuse, probably true, probably exaggerated.

And then the stunt. A throwaway gag, probably thought up over glasses of whiskey on the patio of The Interloper, the bar on Quarterworth Street frequented by journalists and radio announcers and television news anchors. They probably never investigated the legality, considered the health risks. Surely they never thought anything would go wrong.

After it was over, after two hundred and thirty hours without sleep, he left the studio, which was 11 miles from his house, got into a cab, and, as far as anyone could tell, rode off into nonexistence. The driver didn't remember the fare, a detail that was odd in and of itself. Maybe the man jumped into the river from the French King Bridge, or got himself lost in the woods and mauled by a bear. Maybe a dalliance with some underage thing, they took off together in a pinkish haze of new lust, but maybe it stuck. One thing Don was sure of: the guy wasn't a ghost. He was *somewhere*.

Mostly, though, Don was curious, perhaps more accurately rabid, to hear (or at least hear something credible about) the notorious three minute and thirty-seven second stretch that began at 4:35 a.m. on the Monday after the broadcast began. The film's promotional materials indicated only the existence of rumors and unsubstantiated hearsay, like urban legends, a friend of a friend of a friend happened to be tuned in, he didn't remember now exactly what was said, but it was spooky as all-get-out. Some said the segment gave clues about Rampart's then-impending disappearance, that it was a monologue of puzzles and dark hints.

The promotional materials didn't say that the tape would be part of the film, but they didn't say it wouldn't. They did mention rumors of a certain cassette circulated (and, presumably, copied) among high school students in Orford Parish, Connecticut for a time, a tape whose whereabouts were now unknown. Like the disappeared man, that tape and its copies were surely somewhere—under some kid's car seat, maybe, or in a pile of similarly unmarked cassettes under a mountain of laundry in the closet of some metalhead's denim-strewn sty of a bedroom. Maybe at some small town flea market or out of the way record store, in a rack with tapes of prank calls and bootleg concert recordings and demos from amateur garage bands. The thought that maybe the filmmakers had actually managed to get hold of the tape thrilled Don to his marrow.

Now, in the rearview, he could see the white and red

lights of the Civic Center tower rising from the fog tinted yellow of the street lights; above, atop vertiginous stone pillars, the highway moaned its eternally weary moan. Great cracks lined the lower sections of the pillars, and there were spots where the concrete appeared to have been scooped out. In the gravel to the right of his car sat chunks of concrete in patterned piles, presumably gathered and arranged by some of the city's many vagrants.

He shoved the map to the side, gunned the car off the shoulder, kicking up gravel, and continued down the weed-choked street lined with abandoned shacks and lonely shops and service stations bedecked with faded signs; at its terminus he swung the car to the left onto the cracked and crumbled concrete road that led into the warehouses. As a reporter, he knew this alley-veined cluster of deteriorating buildings by reputation only: it served as a meeting place for the shadowy organizations that hustled their wares on the city streets, a venue for gang skirmishes, and a cover for dank brothels of whose workers one was immediately wary, for they looked sickly and thin and bruised, and frequently found themselves in lockup with no pimp nor madam to bail them out. As he drove along the sepia-stained street, he saw at the entrance to a dark alley a sign on which had been scrawled in Sharpie and then written over several times:

The Stay-Awake Man

He turned his car down the alley. At several points, his side mirrors scraped the brick buildings that bordered the unlit lane, causing swirling clouds of red dust to form and dissipate back into the blackness.

The alley opened up into a modest courtyard in which 30 or so cars sat almost touching one another, door-handle to door-handle. He could see no space for his car. He was reluctant to park his car out on the street—the only other car he'd seen had been burnt out and used as a canvas for a variety of graffiti artists. Sighing, he threw the car into reverse and turned his head to make certain the alley was clear. It was not. A man in a black hooded sweatshirt with a yellow vest over it shone his flashlight into Don's eyes. Blinking away the red splotches, he watched as the light bobbed around the back of the car and to his door. The hooded man ducked down. Don could not make out a face beyond the shadow of the hood.

"I've got it," the man said, his voice muffled. Reluctantly, Don opened his door and exited, causing the man to skitter backwards, still keeping the light trained on Don's face.

"You want to point that thing away from me," he warned, squinting, holding up his hand, and the man ignored him and pointed to a grey metal door with no handle in evidence. Don looked at the door, and looked back to the man, but he had already climbed into the station wagon, his yellow vest glowing ghostly in the light from the dashboard. He shot it back up the alley in reverse, faster than Don liked, backed into the road, and disappeared into the darkness. Splotched colors loomed in his vision, psychedelic spatter on the blue-black sky.

Hoping against hope the theater had another sequestered car lot off-site, he trudged over to the door, feeling in his overcoat pocket for his notepad and camera, the latter of which was contraband, as the invitation had indicated that any audience member attempting to record any aspect of the performance would be promptly escorted from the premises. As he approached, the door opened. Don entered past a sentry dressed all in black with a gun on his hip, large mirrored sunglasses covering the top half of his face, the bottom half concealed by profuse and thick black stubble. He drew himself in, expecting to be frisked, but the sentry was still as a mannequin. *The gun, the sunglasses...this is theater*, thought Don, as he looked into the guard's face and saw himself reflected in duplicate, slack-mouthed and drawn.

Just to Don's left sat a bowed card table bearing two coffee carafes, teetering stacks of paper cups, and office-style cylindrical containers of sugar and powdered creamer. Two men in pressed grey suits were helping themselves. They were twins, grey haired, bespectacled, and bearing expressions that indicated they did not wish to be social. A fear struck him that the entire audience might be composed of men who looked just like them, with him the odd man out. Black-haired and thin, with a slight paunch, pools of darkness around his eyes, and a shadow of a mustache—an interloper. He abstained from coffee and decided instead to walk around and get a sense of the venue.

The narrow hall opened into a cavernous room crowded with mismatched folding chairs, some wood, some metal, a few plastic, all facing a large screen on a deceptively flimsy looking metal stand. More chairs lined the walls, separated by squat, featureless particle board tables bearing a fanned spread of magazines, as though during daylight hours the hall doubled as a waiting room. Speakers dangled unanchored by their wires from slits where the walls met the ceiling. A hole in the wall in the back where the brick had been torn away revealed the chrome and black plastic muzzle of a projector. Waitresses in cocktail dresses and towering heels, shapely and red-lipped, teetered this way and that, holding aloft trays of shot glasses brimming with a steaming liquid the deep green of nighttime cough medicine.

Somewhere a bell began to peal insistently, and people streamed in from the lobby and found seats. This was an upscale crowd, Don noted—the men in suits, no shorts, no denim, the women in dresses and modest heels. Feeling somewhat shabby by contrast, Don took a center seat in an otherwise unoccupied row four rows from the front. As the lights dimmed, he put his notebook on his lap and clicked the pen. A small light on the cap made a white circle on the page to write by. Around him he heard murmurs of disapproval.

The projector started up with a whir and a shimmying white rectangle floated this way and that in the darkness until it lit finally on the screen. After a few shapes and zig-zag patterns in various colors zipped about, the screen filled with images of woods in November, the sun shining white through them, blotting the screen, turning the branches to black bones, thin and brittle. The sound of a needle dropping onto a record, loud. Everyone jumped, and a few people tittered. The narration began, a low voice, sounding almost threatening:

Narrator (Voice-over)
Massachusetts Disc Jockey Alan Rampart was a spinner of vinyl records, a radio man, a broadcaster.

Alan Rampart
This is WIDI FM, WLLU AM, the Valley's Voice and the Valley's Choice.

Narrator (VO)
Until everything went all wrong.

Alan Rampart
You can't have animals in the studio, Danny. Danny, what IS that? DANNY. GET IT OFF OF ME. GET IT OFF. (shrieks)

Narrator (VO)
Alan Rampart has been missing for three years now, but the rumor goes that if you drive through his hometown at night…

Jim Ritchie
…in Leeds, Massachusetts, but, see, you have to make sure you haven't slept in at least 48 hours, otherwise you'll get nothing…

Massachusetts State Patrolman Michael Burnston
…but only having stayed awake for 48 hours at the minimum, which is inadvisable, at best…

Jim Ritchie
…and the authorities strongly advise against this, you can hear him, mostly through an ocean of static, but sometimes as clear as a voice in the car with you, somewhere down the end of the dial, spinning records and talking about the madness that pulled him from our world…

Narrator (VO)
…and into the spirit world.

-INTRO MUSIC-
-TITLES:
"The Stay-Awake Man"
Written by Douglas Hathaway
Music by Rip Rippington
Filmed in and around Leeds, Massachusetts
Featuring interviews with:
Jim Ritchie
Mack Burgle
Dan "The Man" Stanton
Finn Morganstern
and more
recorded broadcasts courtesy of WIDI
#
TITLE CARD: "THE STAY-AWAKE MAN"
TITLE CARD: "RECORDING, MARCH 2013:"

Jim Ritchie
…and that's the plan, ladies and gentlemen, live in our studio, from March 15…

Alan Rampart:
…the ides of March…

Jim Ritchie
That's right, the ides of March, whatever ides are, I think they're like drinks, lemonide, lime-ide...from March 15 until he just! Can't! Stand it anymore! our own Alan Rampart will be live, awake, on the air, broadcasting from our studio in Deamon Court, without sleep, without rest, playing tunes and talking about, well, just whatever comes into his tired old head.

Alan Rampart:
Now, how is this going to work, Jimmy?

Jim Ritchie:
I'm glad you asked, buddy. Our other disc jockeys will be shadowing you in shifts, keeping you hydrated, making sure you're not alone, or not alone for too long. Station staff will monitor you on the air, always ready with the seven-second delay in case you say one of those seven dirty words, you know the ones, although I think there are more now. What I'm saying is, keep it clean, pal. You'll have an escort to the restrooms, good healthy food, and good friends ready to jab you in the side with a sharp stick should you start to drift.

Alan Rampart:
I can't wait.

Jim Ritchie:
Us neither. All right, folks, enough jibber-jabber, let's talk March Madness...

As the recording played, snapshots sailed across the screen in succession, stopping just long enough to avoid careful examination: six men in a recording studio, all wide lapels and wider grins, their names in orange italic Helvetica captions across their bellies; a man in a brief bathing suit, sunburned belly and shoulders, straddling a purple inflatable raft in a pool glowing with asterisks of light on a field of impossible blue, holding aloft a cocktail; the same group of men in leaf-patterned short sleeved shirts surrounding some manner of trophy sitting on a table; a curly-coiffed man with a lascivious grin, his arms around two tanned-orange, beefy blondes in abbreviated dresses.

Don's lip curled. He had an instinctive distaste for this manner of broadcaster, for fatuous, unserious, artless men. He'd first seen them in person at WXBK, a television station in Atlanta where he had held a brief internship. They spoke in an unnatural cadence, presumably meant to sound authoritative, *official*, punctuated at random intervals with slight forward lunges, even off-air. Their quips were clichés, their observations trite, and they wore their lusts on their lapels like gaudy flowers.

"Now, we're at 96 hours and counting. Seventeen bathroom breaks. Twelve meals plus a mostly finished veggie platter. How we doing, so far, Alan?"

"Doing great. Hanging in. I'm tired, though, fellas, I'm not going to lie to you. The lights seem very bright. Your voices seem very loud. They bother me, tell you the truth. They make me angry, like someone's having an argument as I'm trying to drift off into sleep. Heh. My own voice bothers me."

"Any hallucinations? Visual, aural?"

"I see…I see a big fat ugly fellow with a mustache asking me a lot of irritating questions."

"Now, Alan, I'm not that fat."

(laughter, sustained, hysterical)

"Alan?"

Rampart's mouth spanned the screen. Thin lips; the tip of a tongue peeked out like a ripe strawberry, slid across, moistening the upper lip. Red splashed across the skin: the

On Air light.

On the screen appeared the words: "Two days before."

The mouth began to move, not quite in time with the audio. "My father used to watch baseball games on television. Something about the sound of the games—the announcers, the murmur of the crowd, the crack of the bats hitting the baseballs—made me so sleepy. Even at that young age, I had bouts with insomnia, and before long the solution hit me. One evening, I brought my tape recorder from my room and put it front of the television and recorded the game. I played the tape every night as I fell asleep. I remember the audio of the game now as though it were the music and lyrics of my favorite records...'...now there's young Thomas, still waiting for the chance to throw out that opening ball. He has been primed and ready for an hour now. This is the young man, you will remember, who was injured in the stands, last month, who got a fractured skull for his trouble, but is back now and ready, his parents at his side, proud as can be. He looks good. It's a bright and beautiful afternoon under a cloudless sky...' It worked. That tape is long gone, now, but all I have to do is call it to mind, and my eyelids flutter like moths."

Now the words on the screen read: "142 hours in."

The mouth again spanned the screen. Now the lips were flaked with dried spittle. They trembled. The tongue, paler than before, zipped across the teeth like the platen of a typewriter zipping back to the left margin.

"May I tell you something in private?"

"Cut it! Shut it down!" someone called out from the back of the theater. Don sunk in his chair, did a half turn, preparing for the crowd to hush the person, but instead the film froze—Rampart's pale pink, pocked tongue jutting luridly out at the audience—and the lights came up. What was this? A fire drill? A practical joke? If it was the latter, was he the only person not in on it? He considered asking the thin, tower-coiffed woman in front of him, but she shrunk into herself, drawing her shoulders inward, as if she'd heard Don's thought and found it mortifying.

A shriek sounded from the back of the room, high and feminine. Don, along with everyone in the audience, looked back. In the doorway shadows scuffled, men whispered. Then sounds of fists hitting flesh, grunts and muttering. The shadows elongated and disappeared as the dust-up retreated into the lobby. When he turned back to face the screen, a cadre of police officers stood in front of it, a few feet beyond the first row of seats. Their faces were occulted behind riot masks, and they held nightsticks at their sides. Echoing footsteps filled the room, and a man stepped out from behind the right side of the screen. He was tall, almost a giant, but gaunt, and bent as though bowing. His hair was white. *A wig*, Don thought, *definitely a wig*.

The man spoke in a syrupy voice, "Ladies and gentlemen, it is with the utmost apology that I must call an end to the evening's proceedings. It has come to my attention that the film shown here tonight contains proprietary material to which the rights have not been legally acquired. The film cannot be shown publicly as it is. I apologize for your having wasted your evening, but this entire enterprise is quite illegal. You may exit the way you came in. The police are here to ensure that you do so in an orderly fashion."

The tone of the man was unctuous to the point of sounding sarcastic, a parody of an apology. Insincere. Don rose, and as he stepped into the aisle, rough hands grasped him by the sleeves and propelled him forward, right over to the tall man. Policemen, masked and silent. Don looked at one, turned his head to the other.

"Are you guys twins?" he asked. They did not reply. The tall man grinned down at Don. The audience murmured as they filed by.

"Camera, please," said the tall man.

"I don't have a camera."

The grin morphed into a grimace.

"I didn't take any pictures," Don said.

The man tilted his head, still grinning, like a confused dog. Up close, Don saw that his flesh was dull white and mottled, like soaked fingertips, his pupils large, barely any whites in his eyes, like an animal. Don reached into his pocket, proffered the camera, a small digital. The man crushed it in his hand as though it were of flimsy plastic.

"Thank you," he said. "You may go."

Don turned to leave and the man called back to him, "You won't be writing about this."

"I won't," Don agreed, eager to be out of there. The man unnerved him, as did the anonymous police. He had noticed that their uniforms were not city-issued. They were black, rather than blue, and bore a profusion of pockets, and epaulets at the shoulders. The badges were shaped like half-moons, and shone in the theatre lights.

Don followed the last of the crowd out the door. He was stuck for a story now, and his curiosity burned like reflux in his esophagus.

The lot was empty of cars, save his own, parked at an angle, the driver's side door open, the interior bathed in soft light. The alarm dinged away, as though the car were singing to itself in the blackness of the night.

The tiles in the studio are changing. They don't think I notice, but I do. I do. It used to be a rectangle adjacent to a square and a smaller rectangle, and next to that, three squares, all in shades of blue, like underwater blue, or white, like the hull of a boat. But now the squares are dividing, the rectangles are elongating. The old patterns are being compromised. The lines between the tiles will be forming words soon. Human words, maybe. Maybe not. Oh, they're not there yet. But they're getting there. And when the transformation is complete, the things that whisper outside will come in. I saw the word "Cohark." Cohark. Mark it. Mark it down. I've got it in my notebook, and now there's a record, because I'm saying this on the air, and the FCC are listening. They have ears everywhere. Believe you me. The words in the tiles have to be right. Stop it. Don't touch me. It itches. You're trying to distract me. I can't forget. Cohark. Cohark. Cohark.

Keyed up, unable to countenance sleep, Don walked the city streets, looking through the grates into shuttered shops, staring at the skyscrapers' tops as clouds blacker than black swam across the sky. He rounded a sharp corner and his gaze was drawn to a row of apartment windows lit brightly, sending a glow into the darkness. In one, he spied a painting in a swirling antique frame. It depicted in blues, blacks, and greys the rough waves of an ocean at night, rows of whitecaps diminishing in the distance. On the horizon floated black amorphous shapes, too far in the distance to identify. Above hung a white-glowing moon, its light ghostly and ethereal. The painting filled him with a hard-to-name longing. He wanted to swim up through the air, enter the window, climb up into the frame, walk into the water, and drown. He yawned until he nearly pulled a muscle in his neck. Then he looked down at the last second and stopped short. A mop-haired kid stood in the sidewalk before him, directly in his path. Don moved to evade the kid, but the kid stepped back into his path He stuck out his lower lip and blew, sending his bangs skyward, revealing a crisscross pattern of ugly scars.

"The tape, mister. I have the tape. Hundred bucks."

"*The* tape? Rampart?"

The kid looked at him, looked around. He pulled from his long coat an unlabeled cassette tape. He raised an eyebrow, an oddly adult expression on a kid who could not have been older than nine.

"Hundred bucks."

Don looked around too as he reached for the wallet in

his back pocket. No one seemed to be paying attention to the transaction. But there were cars parked along the streets, windows reflecting buildings back at one another.

It occurred to him then that perhaps he was being set up, that he'd been followed from the theater, that someone had paid the kid to pass off a blank tape, purported to be a copy of the tape that may contain the missing three minutes and thirty-seven seconds, as contraband. But the kid hadn't said what was on the tape. If it were in fact a set-up, wouldn't he have, so that it was clear that Don was willfully participating in an illegal activity?

What was the worst that could happen?

He paid the kid, who dropped the tape on the road and ran down the street and around the corner. A car that had been sailing along slowly braked, then executed a quick and dirty U-turn, and sped in the direction in which the kid had gone. Don ran to the corner and looked, but kid and car were gone. Clutching the tape in the pocket of his overcoat, he hoofed it back to his car and aimed it for home.

———

"You want to keep the door closed? Every time you open it, more come in. I don't like them. I don't like them one bit."

"Alan, no one's coming in...who do you see coming in?"

"The shadow men. So many of them. So many. Can you ask them to stop whispering? Can you do that for me? Can you ask them? Can you stand closer to me? Can you come closer?"

(weeps softly)

"Please keep the door closed. Please keep the door closed. Please. I'm sorry. Please."

———

Don Wright liked to keep his apartment dark, each

room lit with only one bulb, shaded, in a corner. It had started as a way to save on the electric bill when he'd fallen upon lean times, but he'd become accustomed to the shadows, the fact that his five rooms, with the curtains drawn, existed in a kind of moody half-light. He poured some rye into a tumbler and went into the living room. He put the cassette tape in the player, pressed down the PLAY button.

A voice murmured, unintelligible. Don turned up the volume and a drone filled the room. Alan Rampart's voice, distorted and trembling, sounded from the speaker:

May I tell you something in private?

Then a terrible scream filled the room, distorted, buzzing. The drink fell from Don's hand, the glass landing with a clink on the floor. Rye poured out, soaking the carpet. The lights in the house dimmed…

…and Don woke back in the theater. The screen was still split horizontally by Alan Rampart's lips, the tongue at the center of the screen.

The shriek from the back of the theater. The scuffle in the doorway. The line of strange policemen. Don led to the white-wigged man…and right by him, into the darkness behind the screen. The cops shoved him through a set of velvet curtains and into a dim corridor. He could see a few feet in front of him, but could detect no light source. He moved forward tentatively. Before him stood a door. He took the knob in his hand. It was warm. He opened it.

Who's that?

Don't "Alan" me. That's not Finn. I know Finn. I know Finn's wife. I have lunch with Finn. Coffee breaks. Okay? Who are you? Get your hands off me. Who are you?

Hands. Hands.

I know who you are.

You won't bury me, shadow man. I'll fight you. I have

spiders. Spiders come out of my fingers, see? I fire black widows like bullets from my fingers, shadow man. Undertaker. Their legs unfold like an umbrella opening and they'll kill you with their poison. Shadow man. Undertaker.

That's who you are. Undertaker. Take me under. I dare you. I dare you to try.

Cohark. Is that your name? Is that your name, Undertaker? Cohark?

He flinched. Did you see him flinch? I've got your number, Cohark.

A brightly lit corridor with an industrial-gray ceiling snaked with track-lighting and carpeted in a complex maroon and black pattern. People, 15 or 20 or so, some he recognized from the audience, all walking past. He turned and shuffled along with the group. The hall emptied into a gymnasium with high ceilings and, sitting desolate in the center, six rows of director's chairs with strips of paper affixed to the back bearing names written in black marker. The people began to look for and find their names, to sit. The names were in no order Don could discern, and he was shaken by an atavistic frisson of terror at the thought of being the last one standing on this mute version of musical chairs. He rushed along the rows and the relief he felt at finding his name, three rows in, on a chair nearest the aisle, almost made up for the confusion.

A soft hand lighted on his shoulder and stayed there as its owner circled round to face him. A woman in a black smock. Long, straight red hair and huge eyes.

"Mary Kate," she said by way of introduction, and then she leaned forward until her lips were almost at his ear. He nearly flinched, but caught himself. "You're doing great," she whispered. The people seated in front of Don turned to watch. Their eyes were empty of emotion, unfocused. Mary Kate's lip grazed the outer rim of Don's ear and her breath felt warm on his cheek. He caught a smoky sweet whiff of amaryllis belladonna.

She pulled back and looked directly into his eyes. She began to speak again, and her voice faded out. Don heard clicks and a faint hiss, only the occasional syllable, as her lips moved and her eyes stayed locked on his. It was like a radio station out of tune. Her face betrayed mild alarm. He thought madly that if he reached up and turned her nose, he might be able to hear her again.

Her brow furrowed, a deep horizontal line forming between her arched brows. She shrugged and pulled from the interior of her smock a soft looking brush. She opened a small compact, daubed the brush on its surface, and said "Close your eyes." Don obeyed.

The brush whisked softly across Don's forehead, over his cheeks, the bridge of his nose, back and forth across his neck, touched lightly on his eyelids, back and forth, back and forth. When she had applied the finishing touches, she leaned forward and kissed him briefly but softly on the lips. She took his hand. "Sh…c…on," she said. "Th…eddy…oo." He stood and followed her down the aisle, along the wall, and out into a long, wide hallway. Windowed doors appeared here and there, and in them sat small, dimly lit studio sets: a sandy oasis with a glimmering blue pool ringed with palm trees; a restaurant table draped in white cloth, atop it a bottle of wine and a flickering votive sitting between two elegant place settings with tented cloth napkins and shining silverware; a radio studio with a dimmed ON AIR sign and a bulbous foam-gloved microphone looming over a paper-strewn desk, framed gold records on the wall.

Mary Kate led Don into the radio studio set, sat him in the chair. Above the console was a poster. He recognized it immediately: it was a print of the painting he had seen in the city window. But the angle from which he had seen it through the apartment window must have distorted it. He saw now that it what it depicted was not in fact an ocean, but an unmade bed, sheets of blue rippled and crumpled, sweat-stained pillows hunched where the head of the bed met the wall. Above glowed not the moon, but the shining bulb of a lamp at the end of a curved adjustable arm. He yawned again, covering his mouth with his hand. Mary Kate took his other hand into hers. "It's okay to let go," she said, her voice clear and strong, laced with sadness and, strangely, compassion.

"Thank you," he said, but he said it like a question.

She was gone, vanished. He turned, and the door to the room was gone too. The room was of clear glass, but everything outside it was a blur of industrial off-white, hulking machines, the hint of lights of different colors blinking and winking, like room-sized computers in old movies. Don turned back to examine the console. Was he meant to speak? To broadcast? A sudden exhaustion spread from his heart to his extremities, and the soundproofed walls of the glass enclosure blurred and pulsed. No one was here. Nothing was expected of him. He wanted nothing more than to close his eyes. A face appeared at the window above the console, blurred and ghastly, hollows for eyes, white wig.

Then people crowded in behind the white wigged man. Don watched as their faces painted the glass. They looked so eager, so expectant. Don smiled. Energy flowed into him, filled him up as water fills a vessel into which it is poured.

The crowd gathered in a tight cluster around the booth to watch the Disc Jockey. Despite the black circles under his eyes, he looked assured, confident, comfortable, and awake as he adjusted the microphone, studied the instrument panel, turning a knob here, hitting a button there. The On-Air sign, above him, was unlit. From time to time, he glanced up at it as he arranged his carts, as he adjusted his seat to the perfect height. He cupped his hands to his mouth and cleared his throat, coughed a few times. The crowd sighed, jostling for a view.

Don looked around. The crowd consisted mostly of strangers. But look. Look. Jim was there, and Mack. Dan and Finn, exchanging glances. Mary-Kate, standing on her tippy-toes. A boy with a mop of hair and an elaborately scarred forehead pushing his nose against the glass. Don's wife was there, and his children. How proud they looked! And how relieved! Their faces glowed with love.

The man in the white wig held up two white fists. His index fingers jumped up like gangly puppets. The On-Air sign lit, turning everyone red.

Alan spoke: *This is Don...this is Alan Rampart. My compatriots seem to have left me. I have food, but I don't need it. I pull my nutrition from the flying things in the air. You can't see them, because they are infinitesimally small, microscopic...but if you lunge forward, tongue out, and bite, remembering to pull your tongue back in, of course, you get them, thousands of them in each bite. It really is rather incredible. No one need starve. Isn't that amazing? Isn't it wonderful? Hell, they probably cause cancer. But that's okay. What doesn't?*

Let me tell you about a dream I had, a long and troubling dream. Let me tell you what happened when I woke from that dream

Let me tell you of a thousand years without sleep, and of a sleep that does not end.

Let me tell you about the shadow men. Let me tell you what they told me.

May I tell you something in private?

THE BEGINNING OF THE WORLD

"**W**hat is it, Dad? What's happening?"
I looked hard at Maisie, looked at that sweet, small face, so familiar to me, so real and alive and *present*, saw the candles reflected like flickering stars in her wary, weary eyes. I lifted her up, spun her around, sat her on my leg.

"Sweet girl, sweet girl," I said. My voice sounded foreign to me, low and stricken and hoarse. I cleared my throat, summoned saliva up into the cave of my palate. "It's the beginning of the world."

The five windows, spanning the width of the wall, displayed a shadowed panorama of the city. No lights shone in the hulking buildings, but the windows glowed like a thousand orange boxes, reflecting the low, burning sky. The fragmented beams of searchlights shuddered through them, making the buildings look as though they were rippling, underwater. Higher up, over the buildings' tops, the sky went dark blue, then blacker than pitch if you leaned forward and looked up. This Maisie did. "Are we going to die?" she asked.

"Oh no, honey, no. We're going to be born."

"Born again?"

"No, not born again, not in the sense that the Wickforts say it. There will be nothing to worship, nothing begging prayer, no hymns, no homilies. We're going to be born for the first time, born fresh. And *clean*, sweetheart, cleaner than you are fresh out of the bath, cleaner than your dad when he shaves his beard."

She turned and put a hand on my shaven face. I mimicked biting her finger and she yanked it away, cackling.

There was a calamity out in the hall. "*Motherfucker,*" a voice said, high and hysterical. "Don't you fucking *dare.*" Then the sounds of a scuffle, a struggle, grunting, flesh thumping miserably into flesh. The wall shuddered. A picture fell from its hook, landing face down on the floor. The glass held. I was grateful. I was not yet ready to loosen my grip on my girl.

There was a knock on the door, rapid, insistent. Even before the beginning of the beginning of the world, I did not like unexpected knocks on the door. I gently covered Maisie's mouth with my hand, and she stifled a snigger. Her lack of fear sometimes struck me as somehow alien. I smiled with my eyes, though, and she responded in kind. As foreign, as inappropriate as her cheer was to me, I would never dare discourage it.

"Bricker!" the voice cried, the same one that had been shouting in the hall. "Bricker, I know you're in there. Your car's still there and you goddamned well didn't dare leave on foot. Open up!"

I stayed silent. Maisie and I regarded one another gravely, though I noted still a modicum of mirth in her eyes. The wall shuddered again. The man had fallen against it. We remained still, and after a time he went away, muttering. I heard his door close. It must have been Ruggeiro. I know what he wanted, too, and it was *company.* I didn't want Ruggeiro's company. I wanted to be born in peace.

"Where are *they* going?" Maisie was pointing northwest, toward the mountains. A curving line of red lights flickered like some electric snake in the far dark distance. I laughed. I didn't answer. There was no answer. The city heaves, the world shudders, ready for the dissolution of old life and the bringing of new, and people clamber brainlessly into their cars, driven by the mad idea that somehow *they* will be the survivors. But there will be no birth for them, only death, and death is what they are driving to. *Now* and *Soon* are their only options.

Not ours, no, not us.

Maisie went to the window and put a hand on it, fingers outstretched. Her hands were so small. I rose, my joints popping, and retrieved the picture that had fallen on the floor. It was a picture of Jill, a head shot from her acting days. She was smiling, her teeth perhaps a touch too airbrushed, the curve of her smile just a trifle contrived. My face, reflected in the glass, loomed over it like a warped apparition, a revenant. After I placed the picture back on the wall, I turned. Maisie was staring at me with that look. I did not feel ready for the questions…but we never feel ready for this, do we?

I sat back down in the chair facing the window. She returned to her place on my leg. Outside a gargantuan purple flume surged into the air, roaring like some great beast, then crackling like fireworks, folding inward, turning to pink smoke that undulated in the firelight like a great dancing thing. *Fwoom*, belched the waning world, the old world, the tired world. *Fwoom. Fwoom.* The floor shuddered under my chair. The dishes tittered in the pantry. We gasped, the both of us, a hissing duet, as the windows of the office building to the north blew out. Our candles guttered, some extinguishing, drawing a dismal penumbra over the room. We were getting close.

"What will being born be like?"

I closed my eyes, let the new world speak over my tongue. "Darling, darling, we will ride down a chute of fire, but we will not burn. You remember the waterslide at Wickham Park? This will be like the waterslide, red instead of blue, flame instead of water, but we won't be burned. We'll ride down together, human flumes, careening down into the black warm muck of the new world."

I could see her weighing the merits of her next

question, perhaps fearing the answer. "Why did Mom have to get born before us? Why did you give her birth?"

I looked at my fingernails. I could still see dark lines of blood under the quicks. "Your mother," I answered, "likes to go first, to know things before we do, so *she* can be the one to inform *us* about the lay of the land." I stopped. I knew I was saying too much.

I sniffed back my emotions and started again. "Your mom wants to make sure the ride is safe, sweetheart, and that the new world is one that is worth being born into." I added, "If we don't hear from her, and we haven't, not yet, sweetie, and I've a feeling we won't, then that means all is well. We will be born, she will find us, and we'll all be…"

She was glaring at me in that way that she has, an exaggerated pout, eyebrows held fiercely down as though pulled by strings. "In this new world," she said, and I knew she was going to challenge me here, to try to ferret out what she thought I was talking around - the ugly aspect of what was coming. "can I still grow up to be a marine biologist?"

I laughed, despite myself. "My darling, my sweet. What you will know, what you will learn, what you will be, will go beyond biology. You will *be* that life, that marine life, the avian life, the arachnid and annelid, the human and the alien. Marine biology will feel pret-ty silly to you then, won't it?"

"Daddy, you're just trying to…" and here she began to quote, from her teacher or her mother or who knows who, for she went into a sing-song, made the consonants snap, "put a pretty face on things."

I looked her in the eyes, those green eyes, my eyes, smaller, yes, but my green, looking back at me, and maybe Jill's eyes too, in there somewhere, in the curve of the lower lid, in the sweep of the lashes. "The face of the new world needs neither my embellishments nor my adornments to be pretty," I said. "The birth of the world is beauty in itself, the face of fire, the transference of flesh, the sizzle of synapses frying in a great steel pan. Everything will open up like some great flower."

A crack formed in the ceiling, split, spitting down white dust, snaked along to the wall, whispering and cracking. Sparks, white and bright and innumerable, blinked madly in the fissures. "Our womb can't hold us anymore, my doll, my love." Somewhere I heard Ruggeiro shriek.

"It's okay to scream. It's good to scream. We all scream when we're born, Maisie." I grabbed her and held her back against my chest, my arms tight around her body. I could smell her hair. It smelled like fire, like char. Through it I also smelled her skin, her soap and her humanness, her fragility. It smelled like some blue island. The windows opened up in shards and the walls peeled away. We rode the chute, Maisie and I. Our hair jumped up like birds, and we became sunlight. We rode the chute toward our birth, father and daughter, soon to be twins, soon to be one and to be nothing, soon to live forever in the New World.

ACKNOWLEDGMENTS

The Stay-Awake Men & Other Unstable Entities was
originally published by Dunham's Manor Press in a
limited edition of 150 hardcover copies with illustrations
by Dave Felton

© 2016 Matthew M. Bartlett
http://www.matthewmbartlett.com/

Cover illustration and design
by Yves Tourigny

"Carnomancer, or the Meat Manager's Prerogative was
previously published in Xnoybis 1

"Following You Home" was previously published online
at *The Siren's Call* April 2015 Issue 20 "Screams in the
Night."

"No Abiding Place on Earth" was previously published in
Nightscript Issue 2

"Spettrini" was previously published as a limited edition
chapbook

All rights reserved. No part of this publication may be
reproduced, distributed, or transmitted in any form or by
any means, including photocopying, recording, or other
electronic or mechanical methods, without the prior
written permission of the author, except in the case of
brief quotations embodied in critical reviews and certain
other noncommercial uses permitted by copyright law.

ABOUT THE AUTHOR

Matthew M. Bartlett lives in Western Massachusetts with his wife Katie and their cats Phoebe, Peachpie, and Larry.

Made in the USA
Columbia, SC
28 July 2021

42462273R00062